STORMBORN'S DEBT

STORMBORN'S
DEBT

SHAUN KILGORE

FOUNDERS HOUSE PUBLISHING

Stormborn's Debt
Copyright © 2015 Shaun Kilgore
Published by Founders House Publishing, LLC
Cover art by Melrose Dowdy
Cover and interior design © 2015 Founders House Publishing, LLC

First Paperback Edition: January 2015

ISBN-13: 978-0692384220

For more information please visit
www.foundershousepublishing.com

Published in the United States of America

STORMBORN'S DEBT

1

From the Sea

The tiny boat moved towards the dark shore beneath a quarter moon. The faint light was pale and revealed the barest impressions of trees and rocks. No sign of light from fire or lamp to indicate anyone lived near the lonely beach at all. Two men sat in the boat, draped in thick woolen coats and cloaks to ward off the biting sea winds. One of them moved the oars steadily while the other looked back into the blackness where the ship waited at anchor. No lights again to reveal it to anyone who happened to be watching the water.

A cold, light rain began to fall, splattering softly on the floor of the boat and soaking a bit at a time into their cloaks. Neither man said a word. The only sounds were the waves crashing against the breakers ahead. The boat finally scratched the sandy bottom. There it stopped while the frothing water flowed in and out around them. The first man drew in the oars and waited.

The second man climbed out of the boat and pulled

out a canvas bag. He waded through the ankle-deep water and tossed his bag onto the dry sand. Then he returned and pushed the boat free so it was free to go.

The man at the oars held up a hand. "Gods keep you, Brandin."

"The gods do as they please, Rimley. Just try to stay safe, my friend, especially if you mean to say aboard the Dragonsbane."

Rimley didn't say more but started rowing hard to get past the incoming tide. Under the sparse light, the man and his little boat disappeared quickly. The stars gleamed brightly in the sky and were the only way to make it back to the darkened ship. Brandin got out of the water and turned to stare back out at the sea for some time just to get his legs used to the solid earth beneath him.

After a time, he grabbed his bag and slung it over his shoulder and set out across the sand. He was wearing his old pair of boots now and they made his walking awkward. Brandin was used either wearing lighter shoes preferred by sailors or going barefoot. As it was though, with the air carrying the chill of autumn in it, he was grateful for the warm boots. He left the soft sand in two hundred paces and passed onto stubbly grass that sprouted in ugly tuffs from the parched ground. Though adjusted to the weak light, Brandin tripped over rocks he couldn't see until he was on top of them.

The land grew hilly and he was forced to climb up among the craggy rocks as often as on the softer ground. Darkness made it far more difficult but he wasn't inclined to stay there so he kept moving, one step at a time. It was late enough and by the positions revealed by the charts in Captain Severne's cabin, he was only a few miles from a fishing village. There

Brandin would find some place to sleep and maybe a bit of food if he was lucky. The pouch tucked inside his coat had enough coins for that and more.

With fingers scraped and more bruises than he cared to think about, Brandin reached the top of the hillside and found flat, open country, covered in tall grass that reached his knees. There wasn't a tree in sight for a mile in any direction. Brandin had just enough light to see a break in the flow of grass and could make out the rutted marks of a road when he stepped out in the open. He adjusted his grip on the canvas bag and turned left to head south. That's where he'd find the village. Brandin kept his legs moving despite the pain in his ankles as they rubbed against the inside of the leather boots. He hadn't had proper stockings and none of the other lads aboard the Dragonsbane had them to spare. He'd have blisters by the end.

He kept walking whistling softly to himself to pass the time. It was a lonely stretch of road. Though he couldn't see much of anything, he kept his ears open and caught the lowing of cattle and scattered flocks of sheep crying out. Those he came near to on the road were lazily cropping on the grass and oblivious to any dangers. There was still not the slightest sign of another person. An odd thing with so much livestock around.

The road turned to the southwest and Brandin followed it until the rutted path started down a gentle hill. He couldn't be sure but he thought there were a series of hills rising here and there, some of them covered with patchy grass and scrawny trees while others were bare stone. A goat watched him, making bleating noises until he was well past and turning around a bend.

A cluster of lights shone at the bottom and the sounds of the ocean returned. He could see a sliver of the waters just beyond the village and he could make out the single masts of the shipping boats jutting up into the sky. In the bracing air, he caught a whiff of smoke from the chimneys.

Happy to see the first houses he had seen in more than a month, Brandin started moving faster down the hill, wincing at times when the boots rubbed at his irritated skin. He nearly stumbled but caught himself and kept jogging awkwardly with the canvas bag jiggling around. He didn't see the man standing in the middle of the road until he was mere paces away.

"Ahh!" Brandin lost his footing and fell heavily to the ground, rolling some on the hillside until he stopped flat on his back.

He was breathing heavily and slightly dazed.

Then the man was standing over him with a staff his hand. Brandin couldn't see much more than a few shadows to indicate where his eyes were and his mouth. He seemed to be chewing on something.

"Sorry about that. Just heard something making a ruckus. Then you came barreling down the road there. Wanted to make sure there wasn't a wolf after one of my flocks. They're getting bolder and coming out of the forests to hunt. " His accent was thick and the words ran together some to Brandin's hearing. The stranger reached out a hand a helped him up. "What were you doing on the road at night? Danger thing to do."

Brandin brushed his cloak and woolen coat off. His hood had fallen back. The air was much cooler now. He shivered some before he replaced it. "I'm just passing through."

"Passing through," said the other man. He sniffed the air. "Smell's like you've come from the sea. Smell like salt."

Brandin's eyes widened, but there was no reason to deny it and make the man suspicious. "I came ashore a few miles north. Left a ship now I'm headed to Highcastle."

"Well, I reckon you're harmless. 'Cause if you were aiming to try something, I'd take this staff here," he paused to brandish it, "and thump your skull with it."

Brandin nodded. "Point taken. What is the village called?"

"Garen's Landing. There's a little pub down there if you need refreshing. Don't get a lot of visitors out here so you'll be the talk of the place by morning."

"Thank you."

"Don't mention it."

Brandin was aware of the shepherd wandering off out into the fields. He found his bag and walked down into Garen's Landing. It was a tiny village with on ten or so cottages tucked together there just off a tiny cove. Stout docks held five boats. The waves echoed throughout the stone dwellings and off the craggy hills and brought a bit of the colder winds into the sleepy place too. At the hour, most of the homes were dark and quiet. As he got closer he saw that those spilling their lantern light into the darkness were closest to the pub the shepherd mentioned.

Several mules and a couple of horses were tied up outside the place and Brandin could hear snatches of conversations and drunken singing. The laughter and merriment drew him. The door was closed tight and colored glass let out the light in a dazzling pattern. Brandin pulled the latch and the door came open easily. He walked in and the noise of the patrons dropped some at the sight of the newcomer. The fishermen regarded him warily, their weathered faces made taut by the long hours in the sun, added years. Rich tobacco smoke wafted from cob pipes and filled the place with a haze. The pub was cramp and sported a few tables. The lanterns blazed in every corner to banish the darkness. A fire burned on the hearth and added a sweet smell to the air.

Brandin could feel the tension so he smiled. "Hello."

The stern expressions remain in place. He cleared his throat and to the bar where a ruddy-faced man with a bulging belly that strained the buttons on his plain-spun shirt held an empty glass in his hand.

"New to these parts are ya?"

Brandin nodded. "Just made landfall a few miles up the way."

"You meet Donell, did you?"

Brandin had to think for a moment. "Uh, yes. He found me on the road up yonder. He said I could get a drink and maybe some vittles."

"I suppose, that's true." The bald man held up a hand. "Name's Orley. This little establishment's mine. Welcome to Garen's Landing."

Brandin shook his hand feeling slightly relieved. The action seemed to be a signal. The song and laughter returned and most of the patrons turned back to their cups. To Brandin, it was like the warmth flooded back into the room. He sat down at one of the aged, wooden stools.

"What'll you have then, stranger?"

"How about rum?"

Orley sniffed. "Sorry, lad. I've got ale and a bit of whiskey left."

Brandin thought for a moment. "The ale's fine." Then he

said, "Orley, do you have anything to eat. I know it's kind of late to be asking, but I'm pretty starved out."

Orley came back to him with a mug of ale. He scratched his stubbly-cheeks. "Aye, I can fry you up some sausages and taters. How would that do ya?"

"Very well," Brandin smiled. He took a ginger sip of the ale. It was a bit different than the rum he was used to, but fine all the same. He turned around and held up the mug. A few of the fishermen turned. "Good seas and big catches to the lot of you."

The men returned the gesture and smiled. Pleasant murmurs were filtering through the pub. One of the younger fishers, probably no more than a few years older than he, tipped his hat to Brandin. "Been at sea long, have ya?"

"It's been weeks since I've been on solid ground. I've been at sea for three years or better."

"Been out in the middle of the big blue then? Where the great fish are and the great serpents dwell?"

Some of the other fishermen perked up and listened.

Brandin the rest of his ale and Orley filled it again. "I've seen some big fish; that's true. Some of them are big enough to stretch out from one end of this place to the other. Can't claim to have seen the serpents though there were men I sailed who said they had. Beasts that wrapped clear around the ships, crushed them like pulp, and dragged the crew below the waters."

A few of the older ones were nodding appreciatively. They'd heard the stories with their mother's milk. All fishers carried on the stories. It kept some of the more reckless ones from taking risks out on the open seas. For several minutes Brandin found himself answering questions about life aboard one of the ships that crossed the Casitan Sea. The younger ones plied for stories about the exotic ports he'd been to and asked after the women he'd see in his travels. Brandin told them as much as he could. He made life aboard the Dragonsbane seem a little more exciting and pleasant than it had been. Most of them would probably never leave Garen's Landing for more than a few days at a time to set up at their fishing sites.

Orley came back with his sausages and taters and dropped the steaming platter on the table. "Eat it while it's hot."

Brandin abandoned his storytelling and the fishermen let him be. The sausages were slightly burnt but the flavor nearly made him swoon with pleasure. He hadn't eaten anything like it in months. Dorva, the cook aboard the Dragonsbane, wasn't much on spices and most of his food had been bland and nearly tasteless. Brandin had difficulty not devouring the food quickly.

Orley leaned closer to pour him more ale then whispered a question. "What's your name, stranger?"

Brandin swallowed a big mouthful of fried potatoes. He sipped the ale and wiped the grease from his lips. Orley waited. He was trying to be circumspect about it in case Brandin refused to answer. If he chose to answer, would it matter or would someone recognize his name? He gazed back at the tiny pub. The fishermen were singing softly and puffing away on their pipes. The warmth of the fire was pleasant and relaxing--and his belly was full of fine vittles.

"You wouldn't believe me," he said finally.

"What do you mean? Everybody's got a name, don't they? Why wouldn't I believe ya?"

Brandin sighed. He kept his voice down. "My name is

Brandin Stormborn."

Orley barked a laugh, shaking his head. "No, you're... you're joking. You can't be Brandin Stormborn. You're just... just...."

"Just a man," Brandin finished for him.

Orley's face went slightly pale and he filled another glass with ale and drank it down in one great gulp. He bent closer again, his voice a raspy whisper. "You mean to tell me you're the son Valdan the Stormbringer?" Brandin nodded. "The son of a god?" A few of the patrons turned at the man's slightly animated outburst.

Brandin drained his cup. "Yes. I'm the son of the Stormbringer."

"Well, what do you know. Never thought I'd see the day when I'd have a man with your kind of reputation in my place. That'd be something tell my children about...if I had any." He pursed his lips. "Reckon you'd like to keep that a secret though. Don't want a bunch of folks fawning after ya or asking for blessings and such."

Brandin nodded, feeling a little relief. "I would at that." He wanted to change the subject. "Orley, do you have a place I can get a night's sleep, maybe a bath too. I'm sore in need of both."

"Sure enough you can. I wouldn't want to get the black mark for refusing a quest from Valdan's own." Orley pulled a pendant out of his shirt made of wood carved in the shape of a storm cloud with three lightning bolts coming down.

"You needn't worry about the black mark."

"Well, just the same," began Orley as he cleared away the platter. "I'd not want to be inhospitable on any account now, would I? I have a couple of rooms here. I'll take you once I drive these lads out of here for the night."

"Thank you, Orley," said Brandin though he had doubts the man would be able to keep his mouth shut.

"Oh no. It's my pleasure, it is."

2

Stormborn

Garen's Landing was a place transformed the next morning. When Brandin awoke it was to the sounds of people talking excitedly in the front of the pub. He could hear them chattering in the very back room of the tiny house that was attached to Orley's pub. The pallet he'd slept on was comfortable enough though he kept thinking everything was too still. The motions of the sea moving the Dragonsbane about on the waves had become familiar. While he wanted to ignore them, he knew he would have to face the people sooner or later. Orley had blabbed and now everyone wanted to see the son of Valdan the Stormbringer.

Brandin dressed and walked through the narrow hallway ducking his head so he wouldn't strike the planks jutting from the ceiling. A crowd of twenty managed to squeeze inside and there in the midst of them was Orley. When he saw Brandin he held up his arms and pointed at him.

"See lads. There he is, the son of the Stormbringer. Brandin Stormborn, one of the god's own children and hero

11

among men." The man was preening like a peacock, puffing his chest. The effect was ruined by his nervous laughter. He kept glancing at him, his smile almost slipping. His brow was damp with sweat.

Brandin sighed and walked over. He leaned closer and whispered in Orley's ear. "Well."

The other man shook his head and spoke with the same rasp. "I'm sorry. I couldn't help it. The truth just slipped off me, tongue it did. It was out then. Couldn't stop it. Then folk started showing up at daybreak. I told them to go away, that you didn't want to be disturbed. You was still sleeping at that point. Then some of the lads started asking for ale. I said they could come in as long as they were respectful." Orley spoke with his eyes focused on his hands. Brandin noticed the crowd had quieted a bit as though waiting to see what happened next. "I suppose I'll surely have the black mark now."

"No. No mark. I shouldn't have burdened you with the knowledge in the first place. The fault is mine." Orley slumped in relief.

Brandin smiled and turned his gaze on the rest of the patrons. There were plenty of handshakes and nervous smiles as not only men but several of the village's women tried to get a glimpse of him. Some treated him like a long-lost kinsman and offered to buy him a pint of ale. Even the crusty exteriors of some of the fishermen who he had kept company with last night had faded more and a couple of the old ones behaved like the starry-eyed youths who tried to get a new look at the man. Brandin took it all in stride. It had been many months since he'd been foolish enough to reveal who he was, but the reaction was still the same. Stories about demigods took on a life of their own when circulated by peddlers and acted out by mummers' troupes passing through remote places to ply their trade and get their fingers on a few loose coins.

There were always questions and requests for stories they had heard only fragments of. Brandin sometimes agreed and told tales for an hour or so while wine and food were proffered by whoever agreed to host him. He silently cursed his father. Valdan hadn't deigned to answer even his most strident words. The god was naturally busy elsewhere, much too busy to be a father or any kind of parent at all.

Brandin had spent years cultivating that bitter root of his hatred. He realized that his time aboard the Dragonsbane, traveling from port to port, keeping his head down had cured him of his bitterness. Ordinary folk looked up to the gods' half-children and lauded praises and more upon them. They were heroes of the ages, performing all manner of exploits, conquering whole armies, vanquishing dark creatures that looked like they had crawled up from the underworld. Some were worthy of such honors and obeisance. All but Brandin.

Though his name was Stormborn he had done nothing so great, no exploits for the bards to sing ballads and odes about, no poets scribbling tales for posterity. Brandin hadn't led great warriors on quests by land or by sea to save entire nations. He had kept to himself, bowed his head, and tried to stay invisible. Still, there had been occasions where he acted without thinking, saving villages from roving bandits, stopping a flood from devastating the fields in the country of Geradet, talking King Eshad out of his planned vendetta against King Amenth so that a war was prevented, or bringing down a white lion that had been terrorizing the Incata tribes in Perthus. A handful of incidents, nothing worthy of the attention given by some of the locals. Brandin got away before the grateful people loaded him down with gold and jewels or offered him a choice of virgin daughters.

Thinking about old times, Brandin realized that he spent more time deluding himself than even the proudest of town drunks. His mother had always chided him for his excessive modesty and humility. She was never so closed-mouthed about her son's parentage. His mother wanted all to know she had been blessed with a *starchild*.

Brandin held up his hand to speak. "Please, friends, let's go outside on this fine morning."

The sea air was still bracing but the sun had burned off the child. He had donned his cloak but hadn't worn his coat. The black-dyed wool was sufficient. Brandin stood out among the people of Garen's Landing: he was half a head taller than everyone else. Beneath the wool cloak, he wore a simple white shirt that was made tighter in the arms in the Seneshian style and emphasized his well-muscled arms—a fact not lost on the village's eligible maids. Brandin felt his face warm at some of their suggestive glances, causing him to self-consciously play with his blondish-brown hair. He noticed it was getting shaggy so that it brushed against his collar. Thoughts of a bath trickled through his mind as teasing the locks. Others were drawn to his emerald green eyes, so bright and ready to sparkle with his laughter. He never quite believed they thought he was handsome as any other man might be handsome. Every present was the thought that women only noticed him when they knew he was the son of a god.

The tiny crowd was made up just about everyone in the village. Brandin noticed only one man standing apart. The shepherd, Donell, stood back several paces leaning on his staff surveying the whole ruckus like he would tending his flocks. He occasionally eyed Brandin but then let his gaze rove to other faces. After a time, he turned and walked away. Donell did not seem the least impressed with him.

When the people had gotten their fill of looking at him, asking questions, seeking blessings from him, and nearly worshipping him, Brandin put an end to it. "Thank you all. I will everyone in Garen's Landing well. You have given me your hospitality and I will not forget it. He shook hands again and turned back towards the pub.

Once inside, Orley was there fending them off. "Get away with ya now. The Stormborn needs the rest like the rest of us and I dare say a bite to eat as well." He barred the door and leaned against it, mopped sweat from his forehead, and sighed his relief. "Quite a day. Probably the most excitement this lot's had in generations."

Brandin sat on one of the stools. He drew circles on the aged wood. "Orley. I'd like my bath. I mean to leave for High-castle by midday."

"Oh surely you'll stay another day," said Orley.

"Afraid not. I've lingered long enough. I just want a bath, a shave, and maybe take a pair of shears to this hair."

Orley seemed deflated. "What's yer business in Highcas-tle?"

"Sorry, my business is my own. I'd like to keep it that way."

"Suppose I understand that better now." Orley chuckled. He clapped his hands together and went over to the hearth. A cauldron was boiling. He glanced at Brandin. "I took the liberty of getting the water hot while you were still telling tales."

Brandin smiled, then laughed. His deep throaty laughter

echoed in the confines of the pub. "Good man. Good man."

"I've got an old cast iron tube in the other room there. Might need help getting the water to it though. Me back's not what it used to be."

Brandin walked over to the heath. The cauldron was too large but filled with boiling water, it was much heavier. It hung on an iron frame that let it dangle above the flames. There were two rings, one on each side. Orley grabbed two thick swathes of cloth that slipped over his hands like mittens. He leaned in and grabbed the cauldron and lifted it out. The mittens kept him from getting burned. The hot water sloshed around as he stood up straight. Brandin took a moment to get the balance right then headed back down the hall. Orley led him to another room where the iron tub occupied the middle. There was a stone platform next to it.

"Set it there," said Orley. He stood by while Brandin deposited the cauldron carefully. When it was in place, he took a big ladle and started spooning the steaming water into the tub. He looked up at Brandin. "I usually roll it on a board with wheels."

"What? Then why did you want me to carry it?" Then he knew the answer. The fool wanted to see him display his strength. Brandin shook his head. "Fine. Let's do it this way." He took up the cauldron again and dumped the entire contents into the tub. He dropped it back on the stones.

"Need anything else?"

"No, Orley, that's all. I'm just going to be shut the door and just soak in this tub for an hour or so."

"As you please, Stormborn." Orley's grin was becoming annoying.

Once the pesky man was gone, Brandin sat down on the

chair and removed his boots. The blisters broke open and his feet came out bloody. He hadn't bothered to undress when Orley had finally shown him the pallet. "I really need to get stockings." He sat there for some time just letting the water cool. He removed the rest of his clothes. He sank into the water a little at a time. The soothing warmth spread across his weary body. Once in, he just sat there, submerged to his neck.

Brandin leaned over the side and saw a cake of soap and brush to scrub himself with. He set about scraping away the grime and the layer of sea salt still covered him. He washed it all away and dunked his head and worked the soap into his hair too.

"Gods, it's been far too long since I've had a proper bath."

The air grew clouded with the hot steam so that the edges of the room seemed insubstantial. It was like being in a dream. The hot water was leeching out all of the aches and pains of a hundred days. With his mind open and lulled by the steam, Brandin remembered the last time he had stepped foot inside Highcastle.

He had been much younger then, more awkward and uncertain about himself. He still had hopes that his father was just some traveling soldier or a merchant. Brandin had been traveling for some time already as a guard for Lorn Cosamary, one of the most prosperous merchants in Belandria. There had been terrible troubles with bandits on all the traveler's routes. Brandin had already stood out given his strength and innate skill with a blade even though none knew his true identity at that point. He was worried about that enough to go by the name Brandell Shay.

The merchant trail moved across the winding, dusty roads of the Belandrian interior for weeks to move from one trade center to the next with the capital of Highcastle the final stop. While Brandin had made the trek seven times he had never made it with Cosamary himself. The merchant was apt to stay in Belarush, the northernmost city in the kingdom, preferring to leave his business in the hands of trusted managers so he could pursue other ventures in foreign lands. That trip had been different since he was negotiating a trade marriage that would unite his family with the Bollensi. Lorn was to marry the eldest daughter of Coret Bollensi, a fair maiden known as Breanda. It was not a match made by love or passion, but just another business transaction and one meant to consolidate tremendous power and influence. Despite all of that, Brandin thought it would be just another trip. He had been wrong about that. Terribly wrong.

The memories burned in his chest. Brandin got out of the hot tub and toweled off. The room contained a mirror and washbasin. Rubbing his chin and the stubble he knew he wanted to shave at the very least. He draped his cloak around him and tossed his clothes in the water so they could start soaking. They were in need of laundering. He opened the door and peered out. He could hear Orley moving about the small kitchen behind the bar, clattering pans and talking to himself. Brandin could smell something wonderful cooking although the spices made it hard to know what exactly.

He went to the room with the pallet and undid the cords on his bag and drew out another set of clothes and dressed. He found his straight razor tucked in a smaller pouch with his scant possessions. Once he'd returned to the room he took some of the soap and slathered it on his face. He took the ladle and drew some of the water from the tub and filled the basin. Brandin washed the excess soapsuds from his face and looked at his smooth face. Next, he set about scrubbed his wet clothes and hung them up on the back of a chair. Then he stared at his feet wiggling the toes. He still had no stockings so he walked back to the front barefoot. When he emerged, Orley fumbled with a pan.

"Oh, finished are ya? I'm making some more sausages and some late vegetables, a few carrots, potatoes, and leeks mostly. I hope that's fine."

Brandin nodded. "It'll do. I was wondering if you had some spare stockings you could part with. My last pair were ruined months ago. I never bought more."

The man acted like he was doing a noble service to the crown. Orley puffed out his chest and left the kitchen. "Of course, of course. Anything to help." He returned with a pair of yellowing stockings and handed them to Brandin.

In minutes, Brandin pulled them on. The blisters were no longer bleeding. They were serviceable and kept his feet warm on the cold wooden floor. While Orley continued cooking, Brandin retrieved his boots and slipped them on gingerly. He walked the length of the floor moving back and forth so the boots were in place. The leather was rough on the outside but well made. Far less friction too now he had the stockings.

"I'll be leaving Garen's Landing after lunch."

Orley's smile went sour, but he kept stirring the vegetables in the pan. "Shame to see you go so soon, Stormborn."

"I've lingered here long enough. I have much to do and not all of it pleasant I'm afraid."

Orley didn't ask him again. He knew he wouldn't get an answer. Brandin closed his eyes for a moment and could hear the screams from those long dead now. He sighed deeply sat at the bar. Orley scraped the sausages and mixed vegetables on a platter and slid it in front of him. Then he went to one of the barrels and poured Brandin a cup of ale.

There was no more talking for a while. Brandin ate the meal and thanked Orley again for his hospitality.

"Was nothing, truly. I'm happy to oblige. If ever you pass by my little pub, you can be sure you'll get hot food and a place to sleep."

Brandin finished the ale and went back to retrieve his things. He shoved the still damp clothes in with the rest and cinched up the ties, and put on his coat and cloak. Orley was there waiting for him, a cloth clenched in his hands. Brandin reached out a hand and the pub master took hold of it.

"Be well, Orley."

"And you too, Brandin Stormborn."

The villagers were still lingering around the pub as though they still couldn't believe their good fortune at having him pass through. Brandin a small word for those who came up to him. The rest watched but stayed back now, their own blessings received earlier. Some were superstitious and didn't want some ill-chosen word to undo the blessings they thought they'd received. Brandin took to the rutted road and picked up his pace once he was beyond the crowd crying farewells and blessings for a good journey. He left the cluster of simple houses and started climbing a hill up away from the sounds of the sea. The air was still cool, but he walking fast enough that he started sweating lightly. The stockings were a definite improvement. There was a slight ache from the blisters but they hadn't resumed bleeding. As a result, he could walk much easier.

"You're going to have to get used to walking again on your own two feet," he said softly to himself.

Brandin had covered about a mile on the twisted track, moving up and down through the craggy terrain, straying from the road to walk in the tall tufts of grass to avoid the muddy ruts. As he rounded a bend in the road, he saw Donell standing there, his weight propped on the dark wooden staff. The shepherd just watched him come closer. He said nothing at all until Brandin stopped a few paces from him.

"There were times I thought you would never return. There have been rumors and little else. Then you came back in the darkness hoping you might avoid the sight of the many who've been sent. It was a risk, Stormborn. But then you go ahead and announce yourself thinking no one will hear you. That no one will come to see a starchild."

Brandin looked hard at the shepherd. Something was strange about him. The voice was not right. The eyes were not those of Donell. "Who are you? What has happened to the shepherd?"

"That one is fine for now. He sleeps within while I walk the world of men."

"Have one of the gods come to call on me then? Is it you, Valdan, finally come to speak to me as a father should?"

Donell stood up straight and tapped the staff on the road carelessly, his bearing entirely unlike the shepherd's. "No, Stormborn, not the mighty Stormbringer. He is elsewhere in the world."

"Then who are you?" Brandin dropped the bag and readied himself in case the creature sought to harm him.

"Not a god but those entrusted with delivering their decrees. I'm but a messenger of the gods."

"One of the angeli?"

The shepherd bowed with a flourish fit for royal courts.

"Yes."

"What business do you have with me, angeli?"

"Oh it is an honor worthy of one such as you, I can assure you."

Brandin moved a few steps closer. The angeli remained perfectly still. "An honor? What sort of honor?"

The musical laughter was very strange coming from the grizzled shepherd's face. "Why to serve the gods, of course."

Brandin was angry now at the intrusion of the messenger. "Ha. I'd rather traverse the ten hells before I serve the gods."

The angeli smiled again. "It isn't wise to defy them. You think you are immune from judgment because you have the blood of the Stormbringer in you? Their will shall not be overturned for long."

Brandin grabbed up his bag and stocked past the angeli. "I'll take my chances with their wrath. Tell them I said that."

"As you wish."

After a few paces, Brandin turned back but the road was empty. There was no sign of the shepherd.

3

A Bad Road

The sun was a pale glow behind a thickening screen of clouds that drifted in from the sea that made everything seem bluish gray. Brandin kept moving at a sluggish, creeping pace partly to get used to walking and also because the half-light was making him drowsy. On the road, it was colder too now that he was out away from trees and the warmth that radiated from houses. He was grateful for his woolen coat and cloak. The darkened fabric absorbed what heat there was coming from the sun. He kept his mind focused on the steady plodding of his boots on the rutted track and did his best not to ponder the angeli's words.

"The gods be damned," Brandin muttered.

The miles passed slowly. The fields and hills were mostly empty though Brandin did catch glimpses of sheep clumped together on some of the hills in the distance. After about five miles, he came to another village. There were only five or six huts clustered near the road. Children were running around in the grass behind them while mothers were out in gardens pulling out the last of the season's vegetables so they could preserve them for the winter. The men of the village were numbered among those tending the flocks as they ranged away into the countryside. A stone enclosure on the right contained three plump dairy cows. As he walked by one mooed at him as it was chewing on its cud.

Brandin didn't slow much but kept walking quickly. A few of the children stopped to gawk at him as he passed through but that was it. The village soon faded behind him as he crested and started down another hill. The pastures and fields stretched on for another couple of miles before he descended another hill and saw a much larger town situated next to a smallish river that wound through the lands for miles in either direction. The town had thirty stone houses with thatched roofs. Tiny chimneys blew out trails of wood smoke. Other buildings that probably contained a few shops and even a traveler's inn finished out the arrangement. A bridge arched over the river on two sides of the town. There was an intersection of three paths including the third branch he was on. The other two were covered with a layer of gravel and looked like they had plenty of traffic by foot and cart. The difference between them and the rutted track he walked from Garen's Landing showed how little outside traffic made it to the fishing village or how often anyone used the roads. There were probably many stretches of Belandria forgotten by the crown in Highcastle.

Brandin kept going until his boots hit the gravel roads. There was no traffic on that part of the road but, from the horse dung, it hadn't been all that long. A tall stone signpost stood up next to the road. Words were written on each side of the thick column. Arrows were carved there as well and the pointing to the town said Bell's Gate. The other word beneath it: Highcastle.

"Look's like that's the direction then." Brandin adjusted his grip on the bag again and trudged onward down into Bell's Gate. There were several people out and about at that hour of the afternoon. The sun was much lower in the western sky but nightfall was still a few more hours away.

The people of Bell's Gate were friendly enough. Brandin found himself stopping to shake hands and make other greetings. Children ran in packs through the streets chasing dogs or each other and laughing and shouting their glee the whole time. There were several wagons parked along the street. Men in leather jerkins were busily unloading them while others watched them from horseback holding short spears in their hands. The threads of commerce were thin in Bell's Gate but nonetheless there. As he reached the center of the town, the inn was situated on a crossroads, with each branch heading the opposite direction but both crossing the river just outside of the town limits.

The inn was two stories and made of river stones and cedar. A porch wrapped around the front and sides on both floors and a number of the guests were standing outside, the men mostly smoking pipes or engrossed in conversations. The few women that were gathered outside the inn were trying to be nonchalant about the services they were trying to sell. Bell's Gate had enough traffic from the river to support a modest level of prostitution, though Brandin was sure that it was frowned upon by most of the locals.

He headed straight for the inn, an establishment known as the Walking Groomsman. A few of the ladies eyed him as he walked past them but Brandin did little to elicit more. The day's walking had worn him out and he was thinking that a meal and bed sounded just fine. The daylight would be gone and he wasn't interested in sleeping under a tree or in some shrubs off the side of the road. Besides he had enough coin for several nights.

Brandin pushed open the door and stepped into the warm common room. The smells of venison, stew, and the clinging of stone mugs mixed with the voices of the patrons. It was an enormous room with two fireplaces and two-dozen tables scattered on about the oaken floor. Barmaids moved through the crowds, laden with trays and pitchers of wine and ale. In one corner, a platform rose a foot or so off the ground. On top of it, a woman was singing with a man next to her playing the lute to accompany her. It was a lively tune but hardly anyone was listening. At several of the round tables, men were mired in serious card games or rolling dice. Coins traded hands constantly.

While he tried to not attract notice, Brandin's height and fair hard drew eyes to him as he moved out into the open. Glancing behind him he noticed two burly men standing watch over the common room, their thick arms and broad shoulders stood out beneath their coats. Brandin nodded at one but he just glanced at him before turning his attention back to the tables.

"Welcome to the Walking Groomsman!"

A scrawny little man came up to him, squinting up at him with a practiced smile on his face. "Need a room? A nice meal? Ferendry can provide all at a fair price."

"Yes, thank you," said Brandin. "I'd like a room for the night."

"Very good." Ferendry smiled again and held out his

slender hand. "Ten stars for the night."

"Ten stars?" Brandin gaped. "Why so much? Those pric-es are..." he closed his mouth when he saw the innkeeper's fierce expression. Instead, he drew out the purse from his bag and counted out the crowns. "Yes, well. I suppose that'll be fine. The Walking Groomsman is the only inn after all."

Ferendry took the coins quickly beckoned a dumpy fel-low over. "Orden, take...uh," he looked at Brandin.

"Bradish Gandrey."

"Right. Take Master Gandrey to room number five. It's vacant."

"Thank you, Master Ferendry."

"Of course, Master Gandrey. And welcome to Bell's Gate."

Brandin followed Orden across one end of the com-mon room pasted the hot blazing fire. The logs crackled and popped. He went up the wide stairs and came into a spacious hallway lined with doors. A big window at the end let in the late afternoon light. Brandin walked a few paces behind. Or-den took him to the far end and stopped in front of a door near a second set of stairs. He turned the knob. The room contained a decently sized bed, a washbasin, a small chest for storage, and a chair. A door set in the opposite wall led out onto the porch. The curtains were drawn back to let in the light.

As he watched from the doorway, Orden set about light-ing the lamp sitting on a table next to the washbasin. He turned around once that was done and handed Brandin a tiny key. "Don't have much trouble with theft and such, but here's a key in case you're worried about your valuables or your person."

Brandin took the key. He fished out a pair of copper coins and handed them the Orden. "Thank you."

The man gazed at the coins like he was startled by them. "No one's ever given me a bit of copper for taking them to their rooms. Thank you, sir." Orden left him with a smile on his face.

Brandin shut the door and secured the lock. He tossed his bag on the chair and dropped onto the bed. The mattress was a bit lumpy but the blankets and pillows smelled freshly laundered and there were no mites as far as he could tell. Brandin sat up for a moment and tugged at his boots until they came off. He felt the cool air on his feet through the stockings and let out a grateful sigh.

Then someone screamed.

Brandin shot up again and bounded towards the door, stubbing his toe on the doorframe. He fumbled with the lock for several seconds before it came loose. The scream tore through the hall and a few other doors popped open. Other guests stared out for a moment before closing them again. Brandin winced at his throbbing toe but stepped into the hall. There were sounds of struggle down to his left.

"Stop it. Get out of here!" It was a woman's voice.

Brandin grabbed hold of the door and yanked it open. A man stared back at him, his jaw slack with surprise. He was straddling a woman on the bed. He had ripped at her dress. Her face was red and her lip was swollen and purple.

"Oy. Get out of here. Mind your own business."

Brandin took a step into the room. His fists were clenched. "Whatever you're doing there to that woman, you'd best stop it. Now get off her."

"To the hells with you" The man pulled a knife. "I'll carve

you up real nice then have a go at this pretty one afterward."
Then he jumped down and rushed Brandin with his knife
pointed downwards. "Ahh!"

Brandin grabbed his wrist and stopped his motion as surely
as a wall. The man was startled and he struggled to get free,
kicking mostly since both hands were now pinned. They twisted about in the tiny space of the entrance. The attacker had
stringy black hair and three days of beard growth. The smell
of wine was very strong on his breath. He shoved down trying
to move his knife. Brandin squeezed the wrist then the knife
popped out of his fingers and clattered to the floor. Slowly,
Brandin turned the man around so that he was facing the
opposite direction. The muscles were taut in his arms as he
strained hard to dislodge himself from Brandin's grip.

"Let go of me," he cried.

"If you say so," said Brandin.

His eyes widened. "What? No, wait!"

With a heave, Brandin threw him out into the hall. He
struck the opposite wall and slid down. His head rolled to the
side and he slumped over. Brandin went to his side and checked
to make sure he wasn't dead. The fool was breathing at least.
Leaving him there, Brandin turned back to the woman. She
was younger than he had thought, barely out of girlhood. Her
face was a mess with the bruises and the tears swelling her
cheeks. She backed up against the headboard of the bed and
drew up the coverlet to conceal herself.

Brandin stopped, holding up his hands. "It's okay. You
don't have to be afraid now. He won't be bothering you any
time soon."

The girl wiped tears from her dark brown eyes. Her black
hair was disheveled. The dress was ripped across the bodice

and at the shoulders so that it wouldn't be able to stay up. She looked at Brandin for a moment as though not sure what to say or whether she could get the words out just then.

"Take your time," Brandin said in a soft, soothing voice. "Collect yourself. I can pour you water from the basin over there."

The girl shook her head. "No. No thank you."

Brandin remained there in the doorway. He could hear the ragged breathing of the unconscious man behind him. So far no one had come to check on things. That didn't sit all that well with Brandin. He would have to be a little firmer with Ferendry.

Some minutes past before the girl got the nerve to speak. Her tears had stopped and she had wiped her face with the coverlet. She looked up at Brandin with her puffy lip. "I...I was going to let him do it, at first. He paid me...like...like one of those harlots outside." Fresh tears rolled down the girl's cheeks. "But I changed my mind. I was just so desperate and needed the money for passage on one of the river ships. I can't stay here in Bell's Gate. They'll find me if I do. I used the last of my coins for the room."

She broke down and covered her face in shame.

"Who will find you?"

She looked up at Brandin. "No. I can't say. I won't involve you more than I already have." She leaned over and picked up the coins where they had scattered across the bed. "Please just give those back to that man."

Brandin went to the girl and took the coins. He went back to the sleeping fool and slipped them into his pocket.

"Are you sure you won't tell me who is after you? I might be able to help you. At least, give you money for passage."

The girl shook her head. "No. I will find another way. Thank you."

"My name is Brandell. Brandell Shay," said Brandin. He used the familiar alias though he felt like speaking his true name.

"I...I am Natya Fannis."

"Natya. I am just down the hall. If you change your mind or need anything I will help if I can. Okay?"

The girl nodded. "Yes. Thank you, Master Shay."

"No...please. Just call me, uh, call me Brandin. That's what I go by more often than not."

The girl didn't recognize the name.

"Thank you, Brandin."

Brandin backed out of her room and shut the door. He waited outside in the hall until he heard the door lock. The man at his feet was stirring, wincing from the crack he took to the head. He opened his eyes and gasped when he saw Brandin standing over him.

"You're money is back in your pocket. You'll have nothing more to do with the girl. Do you understand?"

The man nodded slowly. "Yes."

Brandin pointed. "Go."

The man was quick to clamber to his feet and he stumbled down the hall and down the stairs. Once he was gone, Brandin walked back to his room. The door was still open. He looked at his sock feet and noticed a rip in one of the stockings. His big toe was poking out.

"Damn. Wouldn't you know it. Looks like I'll go shopping tomorrow."

He shut his door and locked it again. Brandin went to the bed and dropped on it wearily. He decided to take a nap and

31

then go down for dinner in the common room. "I think I've had enough excitement for today."

He dozed off quickly and woke up to the dim lighting of the lamp. The windows were dark. Brandin rose up, stretching and yawning, a feeling only slightly refreshed. He went to the water basin and splashed cold water on his face. He looked up and saw his reflection in the mirror. His golden hair was long enough to tie back. Green eyes the color of jade stared back too. Brandin straightened up and adjusted his rumpled shirt and coat, taking time to fasten the buttons. He checked his coin pouch and tucked it inside his coat. He left the cloak on the chair and sat down to replace his boots. The ripped stocking was annoying, but it couldn't be helped.

Brandin left his room, pausing to lock the door, and started heading to the stairs. He stopped at the top and turned back to the far end of the hall. "I'll ask her to dinner. She's probably hungry."

When he reached the door, it came open at his touch. Brandin listened carefully. He nudged the door open. The room was empty. Natya was gone. There was no sign of a struggle. The bed was made.

"She left an hour ago, Stormborn. They'll find her though. I can tell you that much."

Brandin spun around and found Orden standing there in the hall. He leaned against the doorframe with a knowing smile touching his lips.

"Ah, Orden, you helped the lady out. You..."

Brandin realized what the boy said. His mouth screwed up in a grimace. "What are you doing here, angeli? Didn't I make myself clear before?"

The messenger wearing Orden's body crinkled his mouth

again. "Oh yes, perfectly clear, Stormborn. Yet you think that this is sufficient for the gods. That there are no consequences."

"What do you mean?"

The sounds of screams and all kinds of commotion carried up the stairs. Then the familiar ring of swords.

Brandin went up to Orden. "What did you do, angeli? What mischief are you about?"

The angeli regarded him with mock innocence. "Just doing what the gods command. The girl has fled and those that sought her are tearing up this inn looking for her right now. When they realize she has been here but only recently departed they will pick up the scent and they will find her."

"And what is my role in this, angeli?"

"Why you are to save her, Stormborn." He laughed with the same light musical laughter. Orden suddenly slumped in his hands. He was asleep."

"Damn the gods, one and all!"

He set the sleeping boy down and went down the stairs. The whole common room had become like an overturned anthill. Silver-armored soldiers were fighting against the patrons, overturning tables, and generally creating chaos. Ferandry was huddling under one of the tables near the bar.

One of the soldiers saw him and pointed. "You? I want to talk to you."

Brandin frowned. "This just isn't my day."

4

A Short Hunt

Didn't you hear me? I said I want to talk to you stranger!"

Brandin shrugged his shoulders. "Sorry, I'm just too busy right now. Maybe another time, perhaps?"

The soldier growled then jabbed with his gauntleted hand. "Get him!"

Six of then men started shoving through the debris, moving past the bodies of the inn's guards, and other patrons who were unfortunate enough to get in the soldiers' ways. They kicked aside benches and tables. Playing cards fluttered in the air. Brandin waited until they were close enough then he grabbed the side of the table in front of him and heaved it up. The whole wood frame came up as a piece. The soldiers gasped. It was a very heavy table.

"Here, catch."

Brandin threw the table right at them. They scrambled to get out of the way, but most of them weren't fast enough. The oaken table crashed down on them. The cries of pain filled the common room. The lead soldier cursed. Brandin turned and dashed back up the stairs. He took the steps two at a time and got to his room. He locked and barricaded the door then grabbed up his cloak. Brandin fished through the bag and pulled out another purse of coins and a small decorative box. He slid them both into his coat pockets and left the rest of the clothes.

With his cloaked fastened in place, Brandin unlatched the door to the porch. Just the sounds of doors splintering and shouts erupted in the hall. It was only moments before they busted through his door. The night air was chilly on the long covered porch. For a wonder it was empty. None of the soldiers had thought to go out the secondary doors yet. Brandin knew he had moments before one of them poked their heads out and caught sight of him.

It was dark enough and his cloak was shaded black so that he had a better chance away from the light. Not that there was much illumination in the town. A few lamps hung from tall poles next to the buildings, but not everyone had them lit. Brandin went to the rail and looked down. It was ten feet to the street. Without hesitation, he climbed over and held fast to the rail while he lowered himself down. There were more crashes above him and he saw lights blossom in some of the windows. Brandin shuffled across the bottom rung of the rail until he was in deeper darkness. At that hour, there were few people out and about in Bell's Gate so it was unlikely anybody could see what he was doing.

Once he was set he let go. Brandin landed hard in his boots. He felt a slight trickle from one of the blisters. Not wanting to get caught before he'd even gotten away, he ignored the pain and ran out into the street. The dirt was hard

packed so he had to content with the soft crunch of the gravel, which sounded magnified in the quiet town. He came to a
smaller backstreet that ran parallel to one of the main routes
away. There were shouts in the distance behind him. Then
there was the metallic sound of the armor clicking and clank-
ing. Brandin looked back the way he'd come and saw torches
flare to life, shining more brightly than the lamps and sending
their flickering light deeper into the shadowy streets.

Brandin jogged up another street, stopping and creeping
past gaps in the buildings. He was moving past a few of the
shops he had wanted to visit earlier. The darkened windows
gave him glimpses of different goods but scarcely anything
else. The route Brandin took wound through the spaces in
the shops and then through some of the houses. Dogs barked
in some cases but he was never chased by them. He kept his
eyes open for any flames. After twenty minutes or so, Brandin came to the end of the cover and stood right up against
a brick house. The road behind his hiding place went across
one of the bridges. Brandin watched for a time. There wasn't
anyone around, no signs of soldiers.

"Got to make a run for it," he muttered.

Brandin took in a ragged breath and left the wall. He raced
across the open stretch of road, the closest concealment a broken down stone wall. He was halfway across when the torchlight came into view. Brandin dropped down. He looked back
and saw that the soldiers were just coming around the corner.
There were probably ten of them in full plate arm, marching
in step. Other men in jerkins carried the torches and walked
on either side of the armored soldier. They hadn't seen him
yet. Brandin crawled slowly towards the short wall, every
moment expecting one of them to see him. He looked back,

the wall getting closer. He saw that it ran largely unbroken to the start of the bridge. The moonlight revealed that much.

When he made it to the crumbling stone, Brandin scrambled over and lay on the other side. "Ten hells, what next?" He knew he didn't want to fight so many at once when he had no weapons.

The river was close enough to hear now, the rushing of the waters helped to mask his progress as he moved along on his hands and knees. Brandin tried to forget the men behind him and kept moving until he'd reached the end of the wall. He moved into the patch of tall grass. When he got to the first stones of the bridge, he went past them and down the slope to the riverbank. Recent rains had raised the level of the waters so that Brandin had to be careful not to slip on the mud and wet grass. The only way to be sure he wouldn't pitch forward into the cold water was to shimmy down on his ass. The cloak was already sodden so it didn't matter. The edge of the bank was uneven, with huge chunks out of it from the stronger currents. Brandin shuffled over until he was right below the bridge. He crawled upwards until he was right beneath the stone floor.

As he groped in the darkness, something squirmed beneath his fingers. The next he felt a flash of pain as he was stuck across the face. "Ow!"

"Who is there?" The whisper was a familiar voice.

"Natya, is that you?"

He heard her suck in a breath to stifle a sob. "Oh, Brandin. Is it you?"

"It is," he said. "I guess those soldiers are looking for you?"

"Yes," she whispered. "What are we going to do?"

Brandin tried to see anything but a bit of moonlight glinting off the river, tried to see where she was exactly. He gave up and stared back at the water. "We're getting out of here."

Natya's voice was strained. "But how?"

Brandin looked around, thinking that they could get on the bridge and cross. But then they would be easier to track once they were out in the open country. The river flowed by, the waters bubbling across the rocks, and then flowing away from the town.

"We should follow the river, stay on the banks and make our way for as long as we can or until we find a boat or another way to cross. They won't be able to follow us as easily if we stay down here."

There was silence. Brandin waited. He wished he could see the expression on her face.

"Okay," said Natya finally.

"Good," answered Brandin. "Let's go now. We need to get some distance away from Bell's Gate." Brandin reached into the darkness. "Take my hand."

After some fumbling, he felt Natya's cold fingers wrap around his. The two of them got up and slowly moved out from under the bridge. The footing was precarious. The mud was slippery and they had to move slowly. There was shouting in the distance that was growing louder with each step. The soldiers were probably searching the town making their ways towards the river. There was no sign of torchlight yet but Brandin winced when his boots came out of the mud with a loud sucking sound. He was sure they would hear the noise and come to look.

Natya lost her footing and nearly pulled Brandin down the slope into the water with her. He dug his boot into the soil and pulled her back. She didn't cry out but only took a moment, holding onto his arms, to steady herself before continuing down the muddy bank. In the moonlight, he could only make out the vague outlines of her form. She wore a cloak too, with the hood pulled up to conceal her face.

Brandin and Natya left the town behind in the darkness, traipsing through the sludge by the waning moonlight. There was no way to account their time by the river, but it was good enough that they seemed to evade the soldiers. Once they were well away from Bell's Gate, Brandin looked back and saw the tiny torches moving about all over the ground surrounding the bridge. He could hear the commands but he knew the soldiers were searching for any sign though they were hindered by the sloping ground, wet grass, and mud. The river was flowing strong just a few paces below where they walked.

"Do they know we went this way," asked Natya.

"I don't know. We didn't think to cover our trail through the mud. They're wearing that armor so they won't be venturing too close to the water. Men weighed in steel don't float all that well. We have a chance to get away and try to cross somewhere down river."

"Thank you, Brandin."

"Thank me when we get away from here."

The uneven ground quickly wore the two of them out. They had to slow down then stop several times to rest. Brandin's stomach growled. He hadn't eaten anything since he set out from Garen's Crossing that morning. When they were stopped, he went got down on his belly in the grass and lapped some of the cold water into his mouth. Natya didn't hesitate to join him. She was as parched as he was and likely hungry too.

After they had had their fill, they sat for a moment there. The skies were clear and a field of stars twinkled down at them. The moon lent the world a bluish cast. He looked at Natya. She still wore her hood up. He couldn't see more than a bit of pale cheek, the end of a pert nose, her chin. She realized he was looking at him and turned away.

"Please. My face." She touched her cheeks.

"Does it hurt much?"

Natya shook her head. "Not much now. He didn't hit me that hard. I just tend to bruise easily."

Brandin didn't quite believe the girl but he didn't want to upset or embarrass her. He sighed then got up. "Let's go."

Sleep sounded lovely just then, but Brandin didn't think about the idea too much. They could make the mistake of thinking they were safe now that the town was gone from sight. They would have to put several more miles between themselves and the soldiers. So far, they had not encountered any other people living near to the water's edge. No docks or boats tied to them to allow them an easy crossing. Above them, the moon moved across the sky until the light broke in the east. The half-moon faded as it gave way to a new morning. The glow increased and with it, Brandin could see Natya much clearer trudging in the grass in front of him.

They had been lucky that the air hadn't turned too cold overnight but he knew it had been wise to keep moving. Brandin still would have liked a hot bath and some sausages right then. He was muttering about breakfast when he saw the horse drinking water from the river not more than three hundred paces away.

He grabbed Natya and pointed. "Look. Do you see anyone?"

Brandin was looking everywhere, but there wasn't a sound or even a glimpse of a rider but the horse bore a saddle with bags attached behind the seat. They walked but slowed down to approach the animal cautiously. Neither wanted to startle the horse and chase it away; if there was no owner, it would be a good way to put more distance between them and the soldiers.

"Brandin, no one would leave a horse like that here. Look at its markings, the work on the saddle. It's a nobleman's horse." She was looking around and around, never letting her eyes stray too long at one point in the grass or among the trees that grew up all around the river at that point in its course. The banks were surrounded by more flat ground before the land rose in a far gentler slope to more fields.

"Let go up that rise over there and see I can see more from there. Stay here, okay?"

The horse looked up and noticed them, but did not move even though it was not tied off. The reins draped on the ground. "Brandin, what about the horse?"

"Well, if you can reach it without it getting too skittish see if you can get a hold on it." He had a thought. "You've worked with horses before?"

The girl nodded. "I have some. My father had them."

Satisfied she wouldn't be in danger, Brandin left Natya and climbed up away from the river. The grass reached his waist in some places. At the top, there were clumps of trees interspaced with raw fields that looked as though they hadn't seen grazing any time recently. Not surprising to find so much open untended land in a kingdom to the size of Belandria, especially when so many young men were lost. The dark memory pricked him.

"Damn it."

"Brandin!"

Natya's scream whipped his head around. Down below, three men had surrounded the girl and the horse; they trained their swords and spears on her. Men in silver armor and leather jerkins. Brandin turned to run down, but someone spoke behind him.

"I wouldn't try anything if I were you, lad."

Brandin looked back and saw a man in his middle years stepping out from behind a group of close-growing maples. He had dark brown eyes and dark hair with a light dusting of gray at the temples. His face was angular and the cheeks were dark with stubble. The noble's eyes were sharp and unwavering. He was dressed in blue linens woven through with silver striping, with a boiled leather breastplate strapped over it. The sigil embossed on the leather and colored in tempera was a seven-tined stag. He wore a sword at his waist and a deep blue cloak draped over it all. Six other soldiers emerged from concealment all of them training crossbows on Brandin. It was then that he saw the stags were cut into the silver armor.

The nobleman looked from him down at the girl. "Hello, Natalya."

Natya lowered her head. She wiped tears from her eyes. "Hello, father."

Brandin looked from one to the other. "You're running from your own father? Gods, why? What could be so wrong between you that you would sell yourself for passage on a ship?"

The words were ill chosen. Brandin knew it at once. The

girl stiffened and turned a fiery gaze upon him. "Yes, some things are bad enough, Brandell Shay."

"What? Did I hear that right? Did you say, Brandell Shay?"

Brandin cursed.

"The gods have indeed blessed me today," said Natya's father. "Not only have I recovered my wayward daughter, but I have captured Brandell Shay himself."

At the mention of the name, the soldiers near Natya turned to look at Brandin. Those at the nobleman's sides exchanged looks of surprise but kept their crossbows pointed at him.

"Ah, I almost forgot to introduce myself. I am Lord Gavin Dungray."

Brandin heard the name but doubted he had heard correctly. A name for the dead, the name of ghosts. "You are the brother of Lord Wilsley Dungray? Wilsley the Black?"

"Ha. Yes, very good. You remember my brother."

Natya was brought up to stand between Brandin and Lord Dungray. She was looking uncertainly at both of them. "Father, how do you know Brandell Shay?"

"Child, I forget that you were studying at the Garderia then. But surely you heard the stories of the lone merchant's guard that incited the Casteny Revolt?"

Natya's eyes grew wide with horror. She shook her head, the hood had fallen back to reveal her raven hair. The bruises were very light and the swelling had gone down some. "No. It cannot be. This man saved me, father. He is not that horrible creature that murdered Uncle Wilsley, is he?"

"Yes, I am."

Both Lord Gavin and Natya turned Brandin. "I am the

same Brandell Shay that struck down the Jade Guards and spurred the revolt that killed hundreds of Belandrians." He bowed his head. "I was going to Highcastle to seek the mercy of the crown by turning myself in for my crimes."

"No," whispered Natya. She turned away. She was sobbed openly and fell to her knees.

"Come, child, you need to get up now. We are going home to Ravenhold." Lord Gavin waved at his men. "Take Brandwell Shay into custody."

Brandin did not struggle. He let the silver-armored soldiers bind his wrists and lead him to an extra horse. He was sat in the saddle and the reins were held by a man in a leather jerkin. His reddish hair was streaked with gray and he had a scar that ran across his chin.

"Prayed to the gods, we'd find you one day," he said in a raspy voice. "Can't believe we found you still in Belandria."

Brandin was drawn along in the line of horses, surrounded by guards. Lord Gavin rode closer to the front with Natya behind him on a smaller horse, her shoulders slumped and her hood once again drawn over her head.

5

The Black Grass

The ride to Ravenhold was harsh and cold. Brandin was grateful for his woolen cloak, but even that wasn't enough to keep the chill winds that swept out from the grasslands that surrounded the road. The country was all waist high grass for miles around them. The caravan had left the river valley and Bell's Gate far behind and passed through farmlands before they came to the sea of wavering grass. Few trees grew in any numbers so there was little to keep the winds from blowing with chilling gusts for miles without end. Brandin was riding among the soldiers, his hands still bound to the prickly bay stallion. All of them were forced to ride in the dust trailing from the carriage that held Natya and her father.

By his vague reckoning, Brandin though they were perhaps another ten miles to Ravenhold. There was little sign of habitation. Most of the Belandrians stayed close to the coastlines of the kingdom, living in the ports and adjoining settlements that supplied food to the urban populace. The grasslands had never been tamed. There were reasons for that, reasons that Brandin

hoped they wouldn't have to encounter. The ruler of Ravenhold was likely prepared for such interference. It made it easier
for Brandin to accept his fate. Still, he wasn't whether his path
would lead him to the courts of Highcastle. Lord Dungray had
his own designs for Brandell Shay.

"Daydreaming of escape, Shay?"

It was the redheaded soldier. He gave Brandin a nasty
smile rapped the bay's rump with the butt of his spear. The
horse lunged forward in surprise, making Brandin wobble in
the saddle. The ropes dug into his wrists painfully. The soldier
laughed and a few of the others joined him. Brandin winced
but kept his mouth shut.

"No chance of you getting away out here. Where could
you run? Besides, you meet a nasty end by one of the..."

"That's enough, Berent. I've heard enough of your gloat-
ing for one afternoon."

It was another soldier who had ridden up on his black
horse. The silver armor shone brightly beneath the sun. His
helmet was tied to the pommel of his saddle. He was a weathered man with sandy hair and gray eyes that had seen many
battles.

"Yes, Captain Kreves," answered Berent. The man saluted
and moved away.

Brandin said nothing as the other soldier continued to ride
next to him for the better part of a mile. For his part, Kreves
didn't seem in much of hurry to speak either though he did
glance over occasionally. The steady plodding of hooves on
the hard-packed earth and the rolling of the carriage wheels
some distance ahead of them were the only sounds for a time.
The wind gusted again bent the tall grass over a battered Brandin so that he had to lean into the wind or else lose his balance.

He wished they would untie his wrists.

"I'm Marius Kreves, the captain of Lord Dungray's household guards."

Brandin nodded. "Hello, Captain. Have questions for the infamous Brandell Shay?"

Kreves smirked. "I figure it was about righting an injustice and it spiraled out of control like a spark catching hold and burning through the brush. But it makes it easier to just turn you into a monster who pushed the revolt until the blood flowed through Belandria."

The truth was unexpected. Brandin looked down at his bound hands. It was too easy to say it wasn't something he chose and that the revolt was just an unexpected consequence. These facts didn't absolve him of the guilt for the deaths of all the people.

He looked at Kreves. "You speak as though you know something about what happened back then."

"No, Shay. I only came to those conclusions in the aftermath when I heard from those at the center of the bloody rebellion, those who were inspired by your quest for justice. I'm no stranger to the ways of nobles. Most of my life I've served the house of Dungray. I served them during the Casteny Revolt. You were praised by the common people as often as you were cursed by the lords and ladies in the courts at Highcastle. Tales of your strength spread. Some thought you were Brandin Stormborn himself."

Brandin smiled slightly. "Fools' stories, surely."

Kreves scratched at the stubble on his chin. He seemed to see into his soul. "Yes, fools' stories. And yet, I wonder. What would they think if they knew the merchant's guard Shay was really the son of Valdan the Stormbringer?"

"Does it make a difference, Captain?"

"Huh, yes it does. To put to death the son of a god is to invite the curse of the gods. Would the king himself risk such wrath let alone my master if they knew the truth?"

"I'm still guilty of a crime. I interfered. I broke the laws and people died. I have to account for that. I've tried to forget, to justify, but I just can find peace with it. I sailed the seas and traveled to distant lands trying. But here I am, back here and ready to pay the price."

"Will Valdan stand by while we kill one of his children? Will he spare Belandria further distress and turmoil just so you can satisfy your need for punishment?"

"Pray to him, Kreves. Let us see what the Stormbringer would say to a faithful believer. I have never had a word with my father. My life has been my own to live. I have never claimed the rights due to me by birth. They can keep their glory. I've wronged so many and I mean to pay for my sins like any other man."

"Well, for all our sakes, I pray that the gods honor your request." Kreves left his side, spurring the black horse into a gallop until he was far up front and lost in the dust.

What did it mean to be known by his true name by such a man and to have him see into the past with such a discerning eye? Brandin half believed it was the angeli again. The creature of the gods seemed bound and determined to bring him to heel.

"I saved the girl and still am on the path that I set, messenger. I will stand before the throne by one road or another. I won't be a puppet. Nor will I be bullied into the service."

Brandin turned his mind back to the cold road, the waving grass, and the course of the caravan. The sky was clear and the sun shone brightly so that the dark wool gradually warmed. It was soothing. He lost himself to the motions of the horse beneath him for hours. His eyes fluttered closed and he managed to doze lightly until he was jolted awake by one of his guards tugging on the reins. The horses and the carriage were stopped on the road. There was no sign of anyone but them. They had passed through a few villages, but they were spread few and far between.

"What is it?"

"We've stopped now, haven't we? Lord Dungray and Mistress Natalya wish to stop and stretch. Should make no difference to you, prisoner."

"You'll get no argument from me, soldier."

The man looked disappointed. He probably wanted a reason to strike *the* Brandell Shay.

He was given a drink of tepid water from one of the canteens the soldiers carried. After some grumbling, he was given a crust of days-old bread. Brandin ate it without comment though he nodded his thanks to the soldier who handed it to him. After a few minutes, he was helped down and allowed to relieve himself. He stretched his aching legs and did his business. His wrists were raw and chaffing. He was escorted around in the grass by a ring of men in brown jerkins. Brandin caught a glimpse of Natya out in the open, her raven hair blowing in the breeze. She saw him but quickly averted her gaze. Lord Gavin paced the road beside the carriage, his back stiff and his arms clenched behind his back. He couldn't hear what either of the nobles was saying but he imagined Lord Dungray was not pleased with the stop. He had a prize in Brandin and wanted to reach Ravenhold with him.

A buzzing noise suddenly reached his ears on the breeze.

The horses whickered nervously, shaking their heads, and pawing the road with their hooves. The humming or whatever it was became louder and it was as though more sources had joined the first. Brandin couldn't be sure where it was coming from but he knew they were surrounded. And he knew by what. The men guarding him exchanged nervous looks and some drew their blades.

Captain Kreves rode back to them. His mouth was twisted in a pained grimace. "Prepare yourselves, lads."

Brandin looked up at Kreves. "They are zeranths, aren't they?"

"Gods, I was hoping we'd avoid them. Some of these boys have barely completed their training. I wonder if they're ready to face them." He looked right into Brandin's eyes. "Will you help us?"

Lord Dungray was hustling Natya back into the carriage. The soldiers in silver armor were forming up next to it on either side, spears and swords drawn in defensive postures. The buzzing grew and grew, coming in waves that rose and were crested by more. A few of the horses were struggling to rip free of their restrains and run. The creatures were terrified. They had every reason to be.

Kreves wheeled his horse around and galloped back the carriage and consulted with Lord Dungray. It did not look like a very pleasant conversation.

A soldier in a jerkin stepped closer. "Hello, Stormborn."

Brandin knew who it was immediately. "Damn the gods, angeli! What now?"

The soldier was smiling in that knowing way. "Still doing the good work of the gods."

"Was it you who flushed out the zeranths?"

"Of course, Stormborn. I needed a way to motivate you to free yourself and defend these men," he twirled the hairs on the soldier's head, "and that fair maiden. You've not saved her yet."

"Saved her? She runs from her own father. I'll not get in the way of family business. Not again."

"Did you not think to ask the poor dear why she would sacrifice so much to be out Lord Dungray's hands?" The angeli held up a finger. "You're not even curious, Stormborn?"

There was still no sign of the zeranths but they were closing in from all sides. The buzzing was breaking up as the first sounds of their fitful breathing could be heard emanating from the grass, which had started trembling with their passage.

"You're just trying to goad me, angeli. I'll not be a fish on your hook."

The angeli held up his hands dismissively. "Then be silent and listen to the others scream as they are devoured." The soldier went limp and slipped to the grass.

The others guarding him noticed. "Osley?"

"The lad feinted outright."

"Ready yourselves. They're coming!"

The bestial creatures called zeranths burst out into the open, on four legs but then stood up on two. They were long and slender with fine black fur. The zeranths' heads were all grotesque features and sharp teeth. From pockets of flesh and bone on the sides of their necks, the eerie buzzing droned on.

The soldiers met the first wave, beating back the slobbering brutes with their blades, spears, and a few well-placed hits from crossbows. Those in the caravan still on their horses charged at the zeranths hoping to crush them beneath the hooves. It worked at first. The warhorses were trained to use their legs and hooves as weapons and they were not as skittish as the other horses in the party. Still, as Brandin watched, they were brought down by a number of zeranths in moments—all while the droning filled the air.

Then they were coming right at him. Brandin closed his eyes and snapped the bonds at his wrists like they were fine thread. The first zeranth lunged at him and he punched it so hard that the creature was flung into the grass where it stayed. He didn't have time to marvel at the ugly thing before three more were upon him, their smoldering eyes and drool-covered jaws hungering for a bit of his tender flesh. Two converged on him simultaneously. Brandin caught both of them by the neck and heaved backward with all his might. The zeranths were sailing end over end and landed heavily. One of them got up for a moment but fell back down clearly stunned by the flight. The third zeranth got him and Brandin was wrestling with the creature in the grass. There were screams and the sounds of the armor rattling all around him and along the road.

Natya's cries came at the instant he snapped the third one's neck. He was up now, his coat sliced and rumpled by the zeranth. His cloak was untouched. The girl's screams urged him to run faster. Zeranths came at him the whole way but he brushed them aside like they were pups, though the force of his motions shattered legs, shoulders, and skulls. Brandin was in his power completely now. The same divine strength that helped him decimate the Jade Guards was with him now. Soldiers fought off packs of the zeranths, but there were so many that they could only keep up feeble defenses. The men gawked when they saw what Brandin was doing or when he came by and left a bloodied zeranth corpse in his wake.

Brandin didn't stop until he'd reached the carriage. The soldiers guarding Natya and her father were fighting valiantly, but they silver-armor wasn't protecting them. Two were down being ripped at by the zeranths. The others were just battering at the rest of a pack with their spears, yet they were getting tired. Brandin pushed through the beasts crushing throats and knocking them aside to get them away from the carriage.

Kreves was there, fending off four of the zeranths at once with his blade. The man was a fine swordsman but even a blademaster couldn't hold off such relentless creatures forever. When he saw Brandin, though, something firmed in him and he seemed like he was filled with a second wind. He leaned into the battle and pushed the zeranths and their buzzing calls away from the carriage a few steps at the time. Meanwhile, Brandin kept hammering at them methodically until the road was filled with their bodies and their blood.

Brandin caught sight of Lord Dungray himself. The man wasn't huddling inside with his daughter. He was battering the zeranths too. Then one sunk his teeth into his steel gauntlets. The lord cried out and dropped his sword. The pack surged at once. Brandin rushed over just as they were descending on the injured nobleman. He cleared them away throwing them away and striking those that tried to snap at him. Lord Dungray looked up at him with a look of shock. His head was damp with sweat and he cradled his right hand next to his breastplate.

"You...you saved me. Why?"

Brandin, hands covered in zeranth blood, his chest heaving, looked down on the Lord Dungray. "I must stand trial, my Lord. To do that, we must all reach Ravenhold alive. Besides, I do not want any more harm to come to your daughter." Brandin reached out his hand and pulled Dungray off the ground. "I must finish this."

He turned back and kept fending off the zeranths as they tried to swarm him. Brandin was beyond noticing anything but the next wave of the creatures and reacting by killing them. It took a moment for him to realize that there were no more coming. The only sounds left were those of the injured moaning softly from the grass. Brandin, soaked through and covered in gore, sat on the ground and just waited for his heart to quiet, his breathing to slow, and eventually returned to himself.

When he looked up, Lord Dungray was just staring at him.

"Gods be merciful. What manner of man are you, Brandell Shay?"

6

City of Ravens

The sea of grass was at its end and the land surrounding the road had become more rugged. The numbers of settlements and villages multiplied and stone signposts directed them onward to Ravenhold. Where there had been no traffic to share the slender ribbon of road that cut through the grasslands, now they were often slowed in their progress by other merchant trains or farmers trucking their late-season produce into the town to see how much they could sell off. The caravan, surrounded by its remaining soldiers, escaped further attacks from zeranths and most of them made muttered thanks to Brandin for their survival. As a result, he no longer wore bonds and rode the bay much easier.

In the aftermath of the zeranth attack, Brandin declared to Lord Dungray that he had no intention of escaping though all knew now that he could have easily overpowered the remaining guards. They had seen how Brandin cut the creatures down. Natya seemed even more inclined to avoid him for the duration of their journey. What else could he have done? Brandin was frustrated by the mischief caused by the angeli but there was nothing he could do to stop the creature. For three days now he waited for it to make another visit or deliver another cryptic message about his responsibility to save Natya.

Another sunny day was halfway over. They traveled along a southwestern route riding past fields filled with workers struggling to harvest the last of their crops. Kreves rode up beside him. He held up a canteen.

"Thank you," Brandin said. He drank the water gratefully, spitting out the road dust before taking several full swallows.

"It's my honor, Stormborn." The captain of Dungray's guards remained beside him, sharing the journey. Brandin knew the man had a strange sort of respect for him now that bordered on reverence. There were some people who saw something of the divine in the half-breed children of the gods and venerated—even worshipped—that spark. His actions out on the grass changed Kreves. Brandin wondered when the man would ask him if he could help him escape his fate.

"Please call me Shay. No one should know who I am."

"Ten hells they shouldn't," answered Kreves. "You saved the lot of us and still you think you need to be punished for a mistake. You're a hero, Stormborn. The kind they tell stories about."

Brandin grimaced. "Why didn't I stay put and become a farmer? I could have just led a quiet life, maybe married, and had a few children too. Would have been a sight better than all of this gallivanting across the known world. Less trouble and less guilt too."

Kreves sighed, his breath a thin cloud in the cooling air.

"Not much comfort in thinking about what could have been. All we have is now; this day, this time."

"Ha. Kreves, you're something of the poet yourself, aren't you?"

The soldier looked at him as they continued up the road. "Might have thought about it myself when I was younger. But look now. I'm here and I've got bloody Brandin Stormborn riding next to me and I've no skills to put the story down in word or song."

Brandin smiled but said nothing more. The caravan climbed a slight rise and then went down the other side. More fallow fields lay beyond with a smattering of huts that gave off light smoke from their chimneys. Further out, due west, rising from behind distant trees, were the towers of Ravenhold.

"Not long now," said Brandin softly.

Beside him, Kreves eyed the same sight. "Have you ever been to the City of Ravens?"

Brandin shook his head. "Never. I'd heard tales told about its towers, but little else. My time in Belandria was spent much closer to Highcastle."

"True enough," said Kreves.

The two men stayed together, occasionally breaking the longer stretches of silence with a comment or two, maybe a bit more musings on things Brandin would rather ignore, before dipping back into silence once more. The caravan traveled until they reached a crossroads. The heavily trafficked road into Ravenhold meant that an inn and small village had grown up along the branches. In the waning daylight, Brandin could see Natya and her father exiting the carriage, the silver armor of the soldiers guarding them shone orange in the late sunlight. If he squinted, he could see the towers, now much closer, but still too far to reach before full darkness.

Kreves halted his horse and Brandin did the same. "A night's sleep beneath a warm roof is welcome."

"I suppose I'll be in the barn though," said Brandin. That had been the usual arrangements since they had left the emptiness of the grasslands.

The captain of the guards shook his head. "No. Lord Dungray is letting you stay inside this time. He said so when I spoke to him earlier today. My master wants you cleaned and made more presentable for our arrival at Ravenhold."

Brandin snorted softly. "I forget that we must worry about appearances. Those in noble houses seem to be sticklers for those kinds of things."

Kreves dismounted his horse and took the reins as Brandin climbed down. "That's something you shouldn't forget from this point on. If it's your aim to stand before the king, then you'll damn well do so in clean clothes and with a fresh shave."

Brandin tried not to laugh at the absurdity of the custom. It seemed so useless or a means to spare the eyes and sensibilities of the ruling class from a life lived on the ground in the dirt. He twisted his hair between two fingers. "Still, I suppose I won't be too upset if someone takes a pair of shears to this hair. I've been meaning to have it cut for a month or so."

Kreves laughed softly. "Well Stormborn, your wish will be granted. Come on."

As he fell into step behind Kreves, Brandin noted that the remaining soldiers tasked with guarding him still kept their distance. When they came within a dozen paces of the carriage, just next to the inn's front door, Natya turned and looked right at him. Her face was much better now. She wore the same clothes as when he first met her, but they had been cleaned and mended somewhere along the road. Brandin glanced at his own dirty clothes caked with mud and other foulness; he winced.

"My lady," he bowed his head. Natya just kept staring at him.

Lord Gavin Dungray turned at his voice. His pale eyes darted to his daughter then back to Brandin again. He reached out his hand and touched Natya's shoulder. "Come, my dear. Let us go inside." She broke contact and turned away.

They stepped up to the door. Lord Dungray motioned to his men and to Kreves he said, "Just watch him. I will have the innkeeper know our business and just who we've brought with us."

The tension seemed to go out of the group as they settled down inside the confines of the inn. The soldiers in armor got the chance to remove it and soon baths were drawn in different rooms of the inn. Those soldiers in jerkins stayed outside the latest, securing the horses and making sure there were no other dangers. After much ado over his presence in the inn, Brandin was led up the stairs to a simple room. A small hearth glowed with a small fire.

"I'll have a pair of shears found and some of the men will prepare the bath," said Kreves. There's two or three copper tubs to choose from."

Brandin acknowledged him but sat staring at the floor. The bed seemed comfortable enough and he was wearier than he could say. "My compliments to Lord Dungray."

Kreves left him there. Two guards were posted outside his room. Alone and no longer moving, Brandin let himself feel the pain throbbing in his legs and back from the miles spent in the saddle. He stripped off the filthy cloak and set about doing the same to the coat too. The dark wool was covered in dirt, mud, and zeranth blood. Next came his boots and the yellowed stocking Orley had given him. He looked at his dark, calloused feet. Brandin could almost feel the Dragonsbane's deck planks beneath them again. He stretched his arms and his back creaked and popped. The shirt was sweat-stained and smelled terrible too.

"Gods, I do need a bath."

The wait for hot water was long. Brandin figured that just about everyone in the party who inclined to wash away the grime of the road took it before he could have a turn using one of the copper tubs. Lord Dungray and Natya were accorded first privileges due to their ranks. Well after dark, Kreves came into his room bearing a tray of a hearty beef stew, hot bread, and a pitcher of wine. The man was out of his armor and wearing a blue tunic. His hair was still damp from the bath.

"They're warming more water for the tub right now. Should be your turn. I thought you might want to eat something. Just about everyone but those guarding you are down in the common room. One of the court bards happened to be a guest. When he learned that Lord Dungray was under the same roof he insisted on telling tales and singing the great songs."

Brandin poured some of the wine into his cup and drank it. "Thank you, Captain."

"Just call me Marius."

The bread was very fresh and the steam flowed out when he broke the dark crust. It smelled wonderful. Brandin dipped a piece into the stew. He took the spoon and ladled out chunks of potatoes and carrots. They were hot enough to burn the inside of his mouth a bit. "How about Kreves? I don't want any of your men to get the wrong impression. That would put you at unnecessary risk. I won't have another's fate in my hands."

"My fate's none of your concern. I'll not have you taking responsibility for my choices too."

Brandin started to argue but Kreves held up a hand. "Just eat your bloody stew, Stormborn. Then you can take a bath because the gods know you stink."

There was nothing to do but obey. Brandin realized he liked Marius Kreves. Yet there were always unexpected dangers attached to being the friend of a starchild. He ate the rest of his stew and finished off the half the pitcher of wine. Kreves waited there for him to finish.

"I have a shirt and breeches that may fit well enough so you have something to put on while your clothes are getting washed."

Brandin stood up and stretched again. He looked down at his soiled clothes and smirked. "Lead on, Kreves. Take me to the tub so I can wipe away the zeranth blood." Brandin pitched his voice louder so the soldiers outside his door could hear him.

The two men entered the hall and the soldiers saluted at Kreves. One of them, dressed in a leather jerkin, stepped forward and puffed out his chest slightly. He was a good head shorter than Kreves or Brandin. "Captain, I can take the prisoner if you have other matters to attend to."

"Thank you, Evens, but that won't be necessary."

Brandin was led to a room at the center of the hall. The

copper tub occupied the space in the middle. A cauldron of water sent up thick steam that obscured the room at edges. Kreves beckoned him in. "There are towels over there. Strip off your clothes and I'll make sure they're laundered straightaway. I've already dropped off my extra clothes for you to wear afterward."

Brandin looked back up the hall in both directions and saw several soldiers posted so he wouldn't have a clear way out if he chose to escape. "Well, I am further obliged to you now, Kreves."

The soldier smiled. Brandin shut the door, removed his shirt and other clothes, and handed them out to Kreves. The man left him alone. Brandin locked the door and readied his bath in peace. In no time, he was submerged and soaking. Time went by and he was getting drowsy when he decided to get out. After he'd toweled off he tried the spare clothes and found that Kreves's shirt was a little tight in the shoulders and the breeches a few inches too short. Still, Brandin pulled them on. When he opened the door, the steam poured into the hall. Once it all cleared out, he saw that the guards were at their stations. They saw him emerge from the bathroom. His skin was tingly and bright pink from the hot water. And the chill that flowed through the hall felt good on his face.

Inside his room, Brandin found Kreves waiting. He held up a pair of iron shears. "Do you trust me, Stormborn?"

Brandin scratched his head. "I suppose that depends."

He let Kreves set to work trimming away at his long, shaggy hair making fast but controlled cuts like he was in a swordfight. In a short time, it was all done and the soldier was tossing the clumps of hair into the fireplace. Kreves pulled a small, bubbled mirror off the wall and handed it to him. "There you are."

Brandin looked at his reflection in the flawed glass. He had shaved his stubble away in the bathroom, but to see himself now, both clean-shaven and with hair a full inch shorter, was a wonder. He looked much younger. "Hmm. It will do, Kreves."

Kreves slipped the shears in his belt and began to leave the room. He paused at the door. "Your clothes will be returned to you and likely mended as well."

"At least I'll face the lords of Ravenhold with the clothes on my back. Gods know I have nothing else now."

"Get some rest. Maybe think about what you'll do once you reach the city. You could always change your mind about handing yourself in, Stormborn."

"Damn it, Kreves. Keep your voice down."

The door shut behind the soldier and Brandin was left by himself in the little room. There was little else do but sprawl out on the bed and try to get some sleep on the lumpy mattress. He turned down the lamp burned faintly unpleasant-smelling oil. The darkness closed in around him. He breathed slow even breaths until his mind fogged. On the edge of sleep, he heard Kreves's words again.

"I'm no one special. Just another man," he whispered. "I must face punishment."

Brandin drifted off.

The next sound he heard was a knock at the door. Morning light shone in his window. Brandin winced against the brilliant glow. "Yes. Come in."

One of the junior soldiers came in bearing a bundle of folded clothes. "Your things." He had a sullen look to his face. He dropped Brandin's clothes on the floor and left.

Kreves came to collect him just as Brandin was stomping

his boots into place. Someone had found him a better pair of stockings and Orley's frayed pair was gone. He looked up at him. "It's time to go."

Brandin nodded. "I thought so."

"Have you thought about what I said?"

"I haven't changed my mind, Kreves."

"Damn it. You should. You really should."

The inn was caught up in a flurry of activity due to the caravan's departure. The soldiers were back in their armor and jerkins. As Brandin accompanied Kreves out into the small courtyard beside the inn, he saw Natya climb inside the carriage. Lord Dungray paced back and forth. When he saw them, he came over and eyed Brandin.

"Well, Mister Shay. Your appearance has been much improved. As you know, my home is only a handful of miles away now. You have kept your word and accounted yourself as an honorable man in more than one way during our journey. I'll admit I am still very surprised."

"Surprised," asked Brandin.

"That you didn't kill us all and flee. I have to wonder what we truly know about the man who incited the Casteny Revolt." The nobleman smiled, though the expression was somewhat cool and did little to brighten his dour face. With that, Lord Dungray left them to claim their mounts from the inn's groomsmen.

Once they were on the road, he said little to anyone but kept staring at the emerging shapes of Ravenhold's legendary towers. They rose out a morning miss that wreathed the forests far ahead. The road was empty at that early hour so they were able to move at a decent clip. Lord Dungray urged the driver of the carriage to put on a little more speed. He was likely anxious to cover the remaining miles. Brandin urged his bay into a canter to keep up.

The day sped by until they had reached the forests, passed through the canopy, and came out the other side. The city of Ravenhold spread out at the base of a valley in which a crystalline lake made up the center. Even from that vantage point, Brandin saw the black shapes wheeling around in the air around the towers. They were the storied ravens of Ravenhold.

Though he wasn't sure what plans Dungray had for him yet, Brandin was willing to accept anything as long as his greater mission was still accomplished. Still, he wondered about Natya. There were questions he wished to ask the girl, but Brandin knew he might not get the chance. That fact bothered him greatly.

7

The Citadel

There was a tremendous clamor in the streets of Ravenhold as the caravan rode down the main thoroughfare. Two of Lord Dungray's men had unfurled banners bearing the stag sigil once they were within arrow shot of the gates of the walled city and the crowds had started to follow along, whooping and hollering, shouting praises to Lord Gavin. Another thing changed when they neared the city. Brandin was told his hands would be bound again. Kreves wasn't at all pleased with the order but he obeyed. His guard was made up only of the silver-armored soldiers, their plate buffed so it reflected the afternoon sunlight. Each of them was positioned around him, their spears held ready to strike him.

Brandin shook his head. It was all theatrics. Word had been sent ahead that they were bringing him into the city. The crowds had exulted at the prospect of catching even a glimpse of such a notorious criminal as Brandell Shay. Now, that they were lining the street, screaming obscenities and curses, throwing rotten vegetables, and horse dung, Brandin let himself absorb all of it. All of the anguish from widows and orphans, the pleas for vengeance coming from the mouths of mothers and fathers who lost their children, all of it touched him and made it easier to ride deeper into Ravenhold towards the citadel. The people would get their spectacle of justice—and how the Belandrians loved their bright spectacles. The news would spread beyond Ravenhold by the peddlers and merchants and borne aloft by messenger birds to every corner of Belandria.

While Kreves fumed silently beside him, Brandin rode with his head bowed, contrite rather than defiant. He had just enough pride left not to play entirely into their hands. When he was struck in the head by a rancid tomato he let the vile juices slide down his face and roll off his cloak.

"Death's too good for you, Shay!"

"May the gods give you eternal torment!"

"Piss on you, you bloody murderer!"

The voices were far worse than the garbage. Brandin took it, drew it into himself, letting his head hang lower, his eyes fixed to the cobblestones below. After a time, the crowds were pushed back by the appearance of other soldiers, more than four units of twenty men. They work thinner plate armor with burnished breastplates with the Dungray sigil painted out in blue and gray hues. They brandished their spears and herded the crowds away several paces so the caravan could continue moving towards a second pair of gates that marked the entrance to the citadel. Brandin looked up at the towers soaring up into the skies. The stones seemed to contain patches of light that glinted and seemed to move in the sun. The ravens flittered about the ramparts where more banners waved in the breeze. The birds gave shrill squawks and some flew low enough that he could feel the wind of their passage. A couple of soldiers were unlucky enough to see white shit on their shiny armor.

"It's impressive, isn't it?"

Brandin nodded. "The ingenuity of men always amazes me, Kreves. Capable of both great good and terrible evils."

"But what of the children of gods and men? Are they not held to a different set of standards? When such beings walk among men do they not stand apart from other men?"

Kreves was looking at him intently. Brandin returned his gaze as they walked through. The doors of the citadel were cranked closed and resounded with a dull thud. They rode into a circular courtyard. Their hooves rang loudly off all of the smooth stones, reverberating and carrying echoes back and forth across the confined space. The guards gave up their pretenses of watching him and they scattered about to dismount and hand their horses to the grooms that were beginning to file into the yard. Beyond the thick gates, the noise of the crowds became muted.

"Why should they be? What gives any of them the right to be treated differently? I am a man just like any other. Yes, the blood of a god flows through these veins," he thrust up his bound wrists, "but I am flesh and blood like you too."

Kreves could tell he wouldn't convince Brandin with his reasoning. "If it's any consolation, Stormborn, you are one of the most stubborn men I've ever met."

Brandin was helped off the bay. Kreves took out a knife and sliced the cords at his wrist. "Come on, *Shay*. I'm sure Lord Dungray will want you to come with him to the Great Hall."

Though he heard Kreves, Brandin was watching Natya exit the carriage with her father following right behind her. She looked back and saw him watching her but in a few moments, she was swooped up by a gaggle of handmaidens in fine gowns and gossamer fabrics who hid her from view as they entered the citadel's central keep. She was gone. Brandin was escorted inside and along tall corridors covered with tapestries, paintings, and other symbols of noble wealth. They meant little to him. Lord Dungray rode several paces ahead of them with his soldiers positioned around him. Other servants darted up and down the corridor wearing smocks and tunics decorated with the sigils of the house. They, too, had heard about the return of their master and the arrival of Brandell Shay in their midst. Most of the servants were able to keep their faces smooth and free of emotions. Some bowed at his passing but most ignored him.

Lord Dungray stopped. He motioned at them. "Kreves bring Mister Shay up here."

Kreves took hold of Brandin's arm and led him to where the nobleman stood with his arms crossed. His cloak and tunic were covered with pale dust, which made both seem gray instead of blue. Everyone else in the corridor seemed to go still, their bodies tense with anticipation. Some were likely holding their breath so they wouldn't miss a single word spoken between Lord Dungray and the outlaw Brandell Shay.

Brandin followed Kreves in bowing. "My Lord."

Lord Dungray frowned for a moment when he noticed Brandin's hands. "Yes, Captain. I want Mister Shay to have guest accommodations befitting his status and importance to the crown. Be sure he has ample security but do restrict his movements in the keep's eastern halls." He pointed at Bran-

72

din directly. "But now, you will come with me to the Great Hall. I have something I wish to show you."

Brandin bowed again. "Yes, Lord Dungray."

Lord Dungray smiled but it was pinched. "Good. Come then."

They were back in motion again, walking down the corridor. More of the household guards closed in around their master and those stationed the length of the passage straightened up and clenched their weapons when Brandin passed. The torches cast tall shadows along the walls, covering some artwork while highlighting others. The images wrought from fabric and tempera were ancient and age had faded the pigments. Dungray was an old house in Belandria. From what he could read on the inscriptions, one name kept appearing in the rolls of long-dead Dungrays: Wilsley.

By the time they reached the Great Hall, Brandin was fairly certain about what he would find inside. The line of portraits and scenes of glory all pointed the way. Kreves marched right next to him, his armor clinking noisily on the flagstones. He was covered in sweat as they entered, his breath shallow and labored. The citadel was enormous. The Great Hall was decorated in lavish fixtures and fine furniture covered with brocaded linens and brilliant patterns of gold and silver threads. Plush pillows and couches were set up again the walls of the room. Four fireplaces ringed the parameter and gave off heat from large oak logs burning inside them.

On the walls, more portraits hung, some in newer mediums, others made to mimic the older styles of the tapestries. Lord Dungray led them up to a portrait that covered several spans and towered ten feet. It depicted a family dressed in embroidered clothes and other finery. The gray-headed man sitting on an ornate chair in the middle was surrounded by a woman who must have been his wife, and seven children of various ages. Brandin knew the man instantly. He was Lord Wilsley of Ravenhold, the elder brother of Lord Gavin.

"You know his face, eh Mister Shay," said Lord Dungray.

Brandin slowly nodded. "Yes, my Lord. Your brother, Lord Wilsley."

There was a fire in the nobleman's eyes now. "Good. I'm glad you recognize him. His blood is on your hands."

"His blood and that of hundreds, my Lord."

"Yes. It is so." His smile was tinged with real passion now. "You've returned to face punishment. You know as well as I do that even now word is reaching across the kingdom all the way to Highcastle. Soon word will return to us here at Ravenhold. You will be held to account. There might even be a trial. I will get justice for my brother, yes. I relish that more than you can imagine." Then he turned away. "But there are other matters at hand. It's what led to our paths crossing. You see my daughter is very special and I had plans for her. Plans that will have to be delayed because of your unlikely appearance."

Brandin frowned. What reason was there for Lord Dungray to be going about all of this? He was his prisoner, not a confidant. Even Kreves was a bit confused.

As though he heard the thoughts, Lord Dungray turned around again, his false smile in place. "Yes, well, I just wanted you to see, again, the face of the one you took from me and my family." He cleared his throat and Brandin saw a bit of moisture in his eyes. "Captain Kreves, take him to one of our guest quarters."

"Yes, Lord Dungray."

The citadel was like no building Brandin had ever been

in. The same stone faced all of the walls and the flagstones on the floor and shone like it was polished marble but yet there were colors and gradations he had never seen. There were patterns cut into the stone and inscriptions written in a language he didn't recognize. Brandin gazed up at the vaulted ceilings and felt the weight of vast age pressing down on him. Then he noticed Kreves watching him as they walked.

"They say the citadel has stood here for three thousand years and that it was built by the gods themselves as a palace on earth."

Brandin continued to admire the handiwork. "Just stories, Kreves. Old ones, to be sure. Another reason to praise the gods. I wouldn't be surprised if one of them spread the rumors in the beginning. Consider the skill, the ingenuity of the men who pulled up this stone, shaped it with their hands, and built this piece by piece. Save your praises for them, my friend. They are certainly worthy of their efforts."

Kreves did no respond at first. He merely turned his eyes back to the walls and ceiling, as they continued walking. Brandin waited but all Kreves did was mutter about him being a 'stubborn, son of the gods.'

Brandin smirked but smoothed his face out when Kreves looked over at him. Kreves snorted. "I saw that." He pitched his voice louder and rougher as they passed another pair of guards. "Come on. Let's get you to your room, Shay."

The guards eyed Brandin as he moved past them, flexing their grips on their spears. He made no indication he cared at all. He walked slightly slumped so they thought he looked broken. In a way, he was though he was thankful, in larger measures, for Kreves's company and friendship. He would probably be the last friend would make before they executed him for his crimes.

They turned down another corridor, one with far less grandeur. It was more undressed stone, with less ornamentation. Not that it was plain by any common standards; Brandin was just as impressed with the shapes of the designs in marble and oak. There were guards in larger numbers, standing in pairs at shorter intervals in front of the various doors.

"The room was prepared in advance of your arrival. The guards quadrupled to ensure security."

Brandin shook his head. "Why didn't they just find me a cell in the dungeons? It's what I deserve, isn't it? I'm an enemy of Belandria."

"Lord Dungray insisted on these arrangements. I know no other reasons for the choice."

They arrived at his quarters. The door was identical to the others along that hall, nothing at all to set it apart from them except for the presence of the guards. There were four posted on the opposite wall and to each side of the portal. They were set at rigid attention, as though waiting for Brandin to decide he wasn't going play the passive prisoner anymore. Though he felt a flare of annoyance, it was tamped down by his resignation to his fate.

Then Natya appeared from the opposite direction surrounded by a train of maidservants and a small detachment of guards. She came right up to Brandin, staring up at him. Her eyes were blazing and her lips quivered. She struck out, slapping him on the cheek.

"How could you pretend to be good, to care what happened to me when you've done such horrible things?"

Brandin met her gaze, his eyes searching hers. His cheek throbbed. Kreves and the other guards were tense, but no one made a move. "I am truly sorry for what happened, though I did believe that terrible injustices were happening in this country, my lady. I await the judgment of the king and will pay for my crimes. You can find some peace in that. As for whether I felt concern for your safety and your need to get away from your father, I leave it to your care to decide in truth." Brandin lowered his voice. "Natya, I do know that you do not want to be here. That you were not ready to resign yourself to your fate. What does your father have in store for you? Why do you fear it so much?"

Natya gaped and tried to respond. Brandin could tell she was having a war with herself about what to say. The presence of the soldiers and her retainers made her cheeks flush with embarrassment—and maybe anger too. She spun around and marched off, her train of servants in tow.

"What was that all about?" asked Kreves.

Brandin watched her until she fled from sight. The questions hung in his mind as surely they must have in hers. Despite himself, the sense of danger surrounding Natya piqued his interest and then began to fester like it always did when people were in need. Though he wanted to claim it as a curse he couldn't bring himself to believe it. *What would mother think if I denied part of myself?*

He sighed then made the decision. "I don't know, but I want to find out." Though he turned and went into the room, Brandin caught a glimpse of Kreves's face. The fool was smiling. He ground his teeth, and muttered, "Damn the gods. Damn them all."

8

Night Fires

Brandin settled into his quarters, which were rather luxurious for what had been set aside as his prison while awaiting the king's justice. He couldn't complain. Kreves stayed briefly then said he had duties to attend to elsewhere in the citadel. The silver-armored guards were left in full force outside the room. This left him time to clean the dust and grime from the road from his skin and clothes. There was nothing else to do until they decided to feed him. Brandin wasn't sure what sort of fare to expect from Lord Dungray. The man confused him and Natya's behavior resurfaced in his mind often in the silence. He sipped water from the pitcher and made himself comfortable on the bed. It was covered in soft linen and stitched with vine embroidery. The furnishings were simple and made very well. Elegant, but subtle craftsmanship.

He followed the patterns of fitted stone that formed a series of lines that ringed the parameter. They were covered in a mixture of colorful glazes. After he scanned the length of his space, Brandin let his eyes drift closed. All of the weariness of the road settled on him and he fell asleep.

A knock at the door awoke him later. Brandin stretched and winced at the tender spots in his muscles. "Yes," he said.

The door opened and two of the guards stepped inside, still in their brilliant armor. Brandin was about to ask them if they were warm inside they metallic skins, but he saw another man enter, garbed in a tunic covered with Dungray's stag sigils. The servant bore a covered tray. He came close to Brandin and set it down on a small table not more than a few feet from the bedside.

Brandin smiled at him. "Thank you."

The man's eyes went wild for a moment. He glanced at the soldiers who were looked back out into the hall. The servant leaned closer. What Brandin thought was fear became something else.

"Hello, Stormborn. Pleased with your accommodations?"

Brandin's smile slipped and he flushed with anger. His voice was low and fierce. "What are you doing here angeli?"

The man smiled. "Oh, yes, I came to see if you were ready to reconsider your foolishness. Answer the summons, Stormborn. The longer you ignore them, the worse off you will be."

Brandin grabbed the man's collar. "You will tell them that I would rather die than submit to their wills. I won't be goaded by the likes of them. The gods are not my masters."

The angeli twitched and struggled to free himself. His mouth was twisted in anger too. "Then be prepared for the consequences, Stormborn." The servant's face twitched and he went limp for a moment. When he revived he gaped up at Brandin. "Help," he cried. "Let me go. He's going to kill me."

The soldiers spun together and clambered in the smaller space to get to him. Brandin let loose of the servant and stepped away, his hands held up in surrender. His shining guards came up to him with spears thrust in his face. Brandin did not move an inch. The servant stumbled to get out of the room and was gone down the hall. Brandin heard the ringing of more armored steps drawing closer. Two other guards crowded at the portal looking inside.

"Is all well," one of them said.

A guard with his spear aimed at Brandin's throat looked back. "He grabbed Gibbs there when he brought him his supper. Made out like he was going to strangle his scrawny neck right there."

"I wasn't going to hurt him," said Brandin.

"Shut up, Shay. Why would I believe a murderer like you?"

"Cram it, Welton. You were there when he fought off the zeranths and when he declared his intentions. Why would he do something as meaningless as throttle a servant in the citadel when he has given himself freely to our custody? Brandell Shay may be a murderer but he's no liar. Come on out of there."

The guards nearer to Brandin still held the spears as though they meant to skewer him like a fish. Part of him wanted them to strike him down but the other part conjured images of those whom he had helped over the years. His teeth ground together but he did not move. After a tense moment, the guards moved away, spears still fixed on him until they were moved through the portal. Once out they closed the door and Brandin was alone again. Steam rolled from the tray through slits in the cover. He sighed and then heard his stomach rumble. While the angeli's words bothered him, he just let them go so he could eat. If something was going to happen then he would meet it with a full stomach.

He ate slowly, savoring each portion until the only thing left was a thin layer of juices from the roasted turkey. He drained the last of the wine from the goblet and sat down to wait. The room was closed off with no windows to the outside so he had only a vague idea about how late it might be. *Surely full darkness had fallen by now.*

The stillness was occasionally broken by the sounds of muffled voices in the hall or other less identifiable noises but what Brandin took for the noises of the fortress itself. A building of such age must continually be settling, the foundations shifting to and fro as the decades passed. He listened to those slight creaks until he heard more voices followed by the rattling of the door and the scraping of the key in the iron lock. The lamplight inside the room had burned low so that shadows danced across the ceilings and the walls. When the door opened, Kreves was standing there, his expression unreadable at first.

"Heard there was a bit of problem earlier," he said. Kreves looked around the room, roved it with his eyes, pausing at the tray on the table before looking at Brandin. "What was the problem with the servant?"

Brandin looked at Kreves for a moment, wondering whether to trust him further. The man was loyal and had kept his secret from his master despite whatever oaths he had taken upon entering Gavin Dungray's service. Perhaps, he could be trusted a little more.

"It's difficult to explain. You see, I've been followed by an angeli since I returned to Belandria. He's been commanded to deliver a message to me until I comply. A message from the gods themselves. This particular servant can take control of people at times, only for brief moments, so he might speak to me with a voice I can understand."

"Ten hells, an angeli. They're real? I remember hearing stories about them when I was a boy."

"Yes, they're real alright. And very annoying. I've wanted to send this one back to the gods with my regards for some time now. I won't be prodded by the likes of him, no matter what."

"Is that wise," asked Kreves. "I mean, they're the bloody gods, aren't they?"

Kreves didn't understand. How could he? He was a mortal man with mundane mortal concerns to keep him centered on the things of the earth. *He wasn't cursed like I am*, thought Brandin.

"That's my decision. I've made my peace with that too. Let them come for me for I will not be beckoned to the Terathic Gates."

Kreves pondered that for a moment, his hand poised like he wanted to speak. Then his expression changed and looked at Brandin. "I went to Lady Dungray's apartments to see if I could find out something."

"What? You did what?" Brandin shook his head. "You shouldn't have done that, Kreves."

Kreves' mouth twisted. "Well, to be honest with you, I didn't get very far with my search though I did my best to get past her maidservants. I never got to speak to her." He held up his hands in consternation. "I was just trying to help."

"Thank you," Brandin said finally. "You do not need to do this. It is an unnecessary risk. You owe me no allegiance, Captain."

Kreves adjusted his tunic, which was made of fine linen and sported the stag insignia across the chest. He wore a quilted undercoat that was made thicker to provide padding when worn beneath the armor. He wore a sword at his hip. Kreves looked every inch the soldier and loyal servant of Lord Dungray yet Brandin realized he was torn between loyalty and reverence.

"I am just a man."

Kreves nodded his head but then shook it. "It's that belief that is stopping you from seeing yourself as you truly are."

Brandin smiled. "More philosophic words from the poet?"

"No, Brandin, I have faith in the ultimate honor of the gods."

"Kreves, it's a waste of time." Brandin waved his hands and turned away.

"You did not mean the revolt to claim so many lives. You've already unnerved Lord Dungray with your actions on the Black Grass. You saved his life and he does not know what to do no matter what he says to you. I have served him for many years and can tell you that he is struggling."

"But what about Natya?"

"Lady Natalya is another matter. I will do my best to find out what vexes her."

Brandin smiled then started laughing. He looked back at Kreves. "Well, Captain, I have to say this much: *you* are the most stubborn man *I've* ever met."

Kreves cracked a smile, ran a hand through his sandy hair, and started laughing too.

Someone rapped on the door, making it shudder loudly. Brandin stood up and Kreves turned towards it as well.

"Yes."

The door swung open and one of the soldiers stuck his head inside. "Captain Kreves, there is a problem outside the citadel."

"What is it?"

"Sir, there are people clogging the streets on every side, calling for Shay's blood. Fights are breaking out and the city watch is having difficulties managing the crowds and keeping order. Captain Henton believes they will riot throughout Ravenhold."

Brandin dropped his head. "You should just send me out there."

Kreves snorted. "That's nonsense. Letting then tear you apart won't appease them. Someone's whipped them up, by the gods. They'll burn the city down in the process." He was moving towards the door but looked back at Brandin. "You will stay here, Shay."

"Hand me over to them, Kreves. It's the only way."

"Captain, maybe he's right. Let them have the murderer. He deserves a painful death." The soldier's eyes burned with hatred. "I was tempted to slit his throat. My grandfather died in the Casteny Revolt."

Kreves hissed. "It's good that you didn't. You'd be tossed in a cell and probably killed by Lord Dungray himself. Shay is his prisoner and he must answer for his crimes and stand trial before the king. Belandria will have its justice, lad." He looked earnestly at Brandin. "Come with me. Rayson, gather three other guards to escort Brandell Shay and have them follow me."

"What are you doing," asked Brandin. "You just told Rayson," he paused because Kreves held up a finger.

"Come out of there, Stormborn." A smile curved his lips. Brandin shook his head. "You fool."

"Come on. Now is the perfect time," said Kreves. "We are going directly to Lord Dungray. You will tell him who you really are."

Brandin came out of his quarters, following Kreves down a series of corridors. The four guards surrounded them. More of the soaring walls and vaulted ceilings opened up and he saw the same ornate stonework, metallic accents, and friezes. Lacquered tiles lit up the floor in myriad colors. They entered a set of corridors filled with sculptures and paintings depicting hunting scenes and portraits of men garbed in the stag emblems of House Dungray. More guards were filling the portals as they walked deeper into the private apartments set aside for Dungray and his family. This was their ancestral home. The silver-armored men standing at rigid attention broke their poses and gave them curious glances. Those who hadn't accompanied the search part for Natya knew who was in their midst. They also knew what was transpiring outside the thick walls of the citadel.

When they turned another corner, the party ran into a crowd of servants rushing around engaged in a host of activities. Messengers bore letters and other missives, maidservants were carrying baskets laden with dirty linens and clothes, and other men dressed in sigil-stitched tunics carried covered trays like the one that contained Brandin's dinner. More servants were busy changing out the lamp oil or pulling torches from wall brackets. The windows were tall and narrow, their clear panes, housed in gilded casements revealed only darkness.

Kreves continued to press on although the number of servants clustered there slowed them down. "Make way! Make way! Business with Lord Dungray. Clear a path, damn you."

Several of the men and women milled around when they realized who had spoken and a gap opened to let them through. Brandin moved along in the turbulent sea of servants but was borne away down the corridor to Dungray's chambers before they recognized him.

The number of guards increased as they neared the main doors. All of them wore the silver armor and held spears in their gloved hands. Brandin didn't meet anyone's gaze but stared at the walls. More artwork covered the surfaces where the stone itself wasn't dressed with ornamentation and engravings. The men didn't know who he was exactly but they knew the circle of guards surrounding meant he was important. They said nothing but did not move until Kreves came up to the iron-reinforced maple doors.

"Are you going to announce me, or do I have to do it myself?"

The man nearest to Kreves gaped and struggled to reach the doors. The captain of the guards had no patience and did not slow up. He came to within inches of the door before one of the guards, a taller man with massive shoulders stepped in front of them.

Kreves stopped short. "Let me by, Commander. We do have business with Lord Dungray. You know who I have with me."

"That I do, and that's why I'm holding you hear until word is passed to Lord Dungray. In case you didn't notice, we have all security on high alert. The mobs outside the citadel are making mischief, Captain Kreves." He pointed at Brandin. "On account of that one there."

Kreves sighed. "Let him know that we are here then."

The echo of armored boots pounding the stone floors reached them a few moments before a whole squad of soldiers in leather jerkins turned down the hall. They were jogging directly towards them. One of the soldiers saluted Kreves and the Commander barring the door.

"Urgent message from the city watch commander for Lord Dungray. Captain Kreves, we are getting reports of fires in and around the Matron's Quarter. Crews have been dispatched to try to contain the fire and ascertain who is responsible. There are at least five confirmed blazes. "

"Damn it," growled Kreves.

Brandin shook his head. *The angeli's work.* "It has to be."

"What? What does it have to be," asked Kreves.

He was surrounded by a ring of strangers who did not know who he was. Did not know what sort of danger the angeli could pose since he was frustrated in his work.

The doors squealed in protest behind them, opening slowly and revealing how thick the maple had been cut to make the entrance to the noble's apartments. Standing in the middle of the portal was Dungray himself, his arms crossed and his expression severe. "What is happening out here? I will have order by the gods."

"It's the gods that you should be concerned about, Lord Dungray," said Brandin. His voice carried all of the frustration and intensity he felt. Dungray saw him and returned his gaze, though his cheek twitched and his eyes darted from Brandin to the soldiers crowding in around them.

"What are you talking about, Shay? The gods? What of them? Captain Kreves, why do you bring this criminal to my door at this serious hour?"

"My lord," Kreves began.

Brandin stepped forward. "I speak of the gods because one of their messengers plays games with your people, Lord Dungray. Even now, the angeli spreads out his web of mischief and the city begins to burn."

"How do you know this, Shay? Why do I believe you?" There was something in his eyes, maybe recognition, maybe fear. Brandin wasn't sure. Maybe he didn't care.

"I know because I am starborn."

Some of the soldiers gasped while others snorted derisively, muttering that he was a madman and murderer. Kreves bowed his head. Brandin did not fault the man. With the angeli at work, he had no choice but to reveal who he was. Dungray stared at him, not daring to blink.

"You? A child of the gods? One of the half-blood spawns?"

"I am Brandin Stormborn, my lord."

"What did he say," asked one of the men.

Another voice piped up. "He said he was Stormborn."

Then another answered. "Then doesn't that make him the son of the Stormbringer?"

Brandin spoke loudly in the confined space in front of the portal. "I am the son of Valdan the Stormbringer, the god of the sea and storms."

Dungray stared on, his mouth poised to say something but he was unable to speak it.

"What? You're a child of the gods? A true demigod?"

It was Natya's voice. Brandin redirected his eyes to where the girl stood with her entourage further back inside the apartments. The maidservants were all fluttery-eyed and giggling amongst one another. *They were ready to scurry in fear when they saw me only as Shay.* The display unnerved Brandin.

"Go back to your room, Natalya."

"No." She stiffened her back in defiance.

Lord Dungray's mouth twisted and then his face contorted in fury. "What did you say?"

Brandin started at the girl, her dark hair almost bristling with rage. "I said no, father. I will not listen." Natya's expression softened when she turned her eyes on him. Some of the warmth and gratitude was there again. "Brandin," she started, but paused. "That is your name?"

"Yes, my lady," said Brandin.

"Brandin Stormborn, though I would wish to hear how you became associated with the name Brandell Shay, I have something to ask of you."

Lord Dungray and his men seemed spellbound. Brandin glanced at Kreves and the man looked almost relieved. He wouldn't have to tease out the meaning of Natya's distress after all.

"I would ask you to deliver me from a terrible fate."

"Natalya, please," Dungray begged.

She carried on as though he had said nothing. "My father has decided that the only way to save us all is to hand me over to...to a monster, a creature known to us only as Oracandus. Please, help me. Please save me."

There was a quiet in that hall before the giant maple doors that became deeper than a tomb's silence. No one dared breathed. The sounds of servants moving down the hall seemed unnaturally muffled. Brandin looked Lord Dungray and Natalya. He wondered if they were just pawns in a game of the gods set up just for him. The old guilt ached in his heart. All of those dead Belandrians spurred on by his words and his deeds. Now, before him was someone in dire need. It made his surrender seem pathetic and self-serving. Brandin gritted his teeth. "I will help you, Natya." The girl looked relieved and tears bloomed in her eyes. He turned his fiery gaze on Lord Dungray. "But first you must tell me of your pact with this Oracandus."

9

The Beast

Lord Dungray looked drained and deflated. His earlier anger spent, he looked at the guards surrounding them. "Leave us. Return to your posts. I need reports on what is happening in the city. I want things back under control."

The soldiers jumped to obey. Kreves seemed to know he wasn't included in the order or he was he chose to ignore it. Brandin was grateful he was staying. Over half the soldiers cleared away leaving only the two or three on duty near the entrance the apartments and those assigned to Natya. Lord Dungray moved through the door, pausing to look back when Brandin stayed where he was, wincing as though in pain.

"Please, come inside. I will tell you what I know of Oracandus." He glanced at Natya as he continued deeper into their apartments.

Brandin and Kreves followed behind and the heavy maple doors closed behind them. The hall was lit brightly with gilded brass lamps with colored glass shades. The walls were covered with patterned panels and portraits like those Dungray showed him when he had first arrived. The richness of the furnishings surpassed that out in the public areas of the citadel, representing just a tiny portion of the wealth held by the Dungray household. The Lord of Ravenhold led them to a formal sitting room replete with plush couches, a table, and ladder-back chairs, and fire glowing small in the hearth of an enormous fireplace.

Dungray went to one of the couches and sat down heavily. Servants appeared from an alcove bearing wine on silver trays. Natya drifted in and took a seat on the opposite couch. She shooed her maidservants away. The ladies were pale and shaking, thanking her profusely for dismissing them.

Kreves came up beside Brandin. Dungray noticed the look that passed between them. "It seems you've already garnered loyalty from my Captain, Brandin Stormborn." He shook his head and stared at a place on the wall for a moment. "You claim to be the son of a god, one of the starborn we hear stories about. You also say you are Brandell Shay, the man responsible for the deaths of many including my brother."

"I am both," said Brandin.

Dungray wiped his brow. "I had no choice but to make an arrangement with the Oracandus, you know." He gave Natya a pained look. "He came to us in the guise of an outlander noble, one filled with the arrogance of his title. I rejected the offer, such as it was. He insisted we would pay for our refusal." At this point, Dungray stopped, wiped the sweat from his brow. "I sent assassins to deal with him."

"Oh, father!" Natya gasped. "Why didn't you tell me?"

"When he was attacked, Oracandus revealed himself for the monster he truly is and attacked our men and went after several of the southern villages. Word was sent to Ravenhold that if we did not give him Natalya not even the armies of Highcastle could prevail against him."

"You believed his threats," asked Brandin.

"Yes. He killed every man, woman, and child in two villages and decimated the militias too. Not one man left standing." Dungray slumped in his seat. "I'm so sorry, Natalya."

"So you agreed to the marriage to prevent further deaths? And you did not alert the king to what was happening in and around Ravenhold?"

"Yes," said Dungray.

Brandin approached the table where the wine had been left. He poured himself a cup and drank it slowly. He turned around and walked towards the hearth, thinking and considering courses of action. There was only one definitive answer and Brandin wasn't very pleased with it. He turned back to the others. "I will have to confront this Oracandus and defeat him. That's the only way I can save Natya and secure Ravenhold." He didn't add out loud that it would be a means to make amends but had a feeling Dungray might see it that way too.

"Are you truly Brandin Stormborn?" Dungray's eyes were haunted but he strained to look directly at Brandin.

"I am. It is as much a curse as it is a blessing. Will you let me help you?"

The nobleman leaned over so his elbows rested on his knees. All of the arrogance he showed at their previous meetings was gone. Sweat beaded on his forehead, his hair was disheveled. It had all been pretense up until they reached Ravenhold. Brandin recognized it all then drained down the rest of his wine. Kreves was still standing by, not engaging in the conversation at all. He was probably considering his actions up until this point. He was a fool if wasn't doing that very thing. Brandin sighed. From time to time, people were caught in the vortex of his presence like he was a sinking ship pulling them under the waves. Perhaps the influence of the starchild. Whatever it was, Brandin did not like the results most of the time. Still, Kreves was an exception.

"Where can I find Oracandus?"

Dungray blinked. He started to speak but a rasping sound came out. The nobleman coughed to clear his throat. Natya went to the table and poured her father a cup of wine. Dungray drank it all at once. "Thank you, my dear." He seemed less shaky. "He is living in the forests just beyond the city. Close enough to keep the threats palpable. From time to time, he attacks merchant wagons or farmers bringing produce to market."

Brandin nodded. He scratched at the stubble on his chin. He walked back over to Kreves. He looked at him. "How did you not know of this?"

Before he could answer Lord Dungray spoke.

"Only those in my elite guards were given knowledge of Oracandus. Everyone else assumed I was negotiating a common marriage contract...and Natalya did not agree with my decision. Captain Kreves was brought in only when she fled the city."

Natya wiped fresh tears from her cheeks but said nothing. Brandin paced back and forth, occasionally looking at her and Kreves. Across the room, he could see the blackness of night reaching in through the casement windows. He sniffed and caught a whiff of smoke. The city still burned. The angeli. He wanted to strangle the creature and throw him at the feet of the gods in their celestial halls.

"Take me to the beast."

Dungray sat up straight. "Will you do this, truly?"

"Yes, Lord Dungray. I will do it. Maybe I need to do it."

Dungray nodded, his expression turned thoughtful. "I said it before, but I will say it again. You are no ordinary man. For Natalya's life, I will forget the life you took. Once that creature is dead, you are free. I swear by the gods, one and all." The nobleman smiled, a slight curving his lips.

"That is more than I deserve."

Kreves was smiling now. "See. I told you that telling him the truth was the right course."

Brandin shook his head. "Yes, I see now. You've got Brandin bloody Stormborn in your midst. Can we try to keep it to yourselves?"

"It's settled then," said Dungray. "You will set out for the forests in the morning. Kreves, I'm sure you want to be included so you can lead the troops that I send along with him."

"Yes, my lord." The salute came a second later. "Lord Dungray."

"Please, take one of the guest rooms here instead of returning to your quarters." Dungray reached for a small bell that was perched on one of the cushions and jingled it. The light, twinkling sound was immediately answered by servants who reappeared from the doors set in the alcove. A woman servant curtsied low. "My lord?"

"Ilsa, take this man to one of our guest rooms and attend to his needs."

"As you command," Ilsa curtsied again and motioned for Brandin to follow her down one of the side corridors that branched off from the main sitting room.

Brandin nodded and followed Ilsa away from the sitting room. The hour was very late and weariness was pulling his eyelids down. He yawned so wide his mouth ached. Ilsa padded down the hall very slowly. Brandin noticed no guards were lining the wall on that branch and the lighting was softer from less torchlight. Ilsa stopped at one of the doors and retrieved a lamp from a table and used the nearest torch to light the wick. Once it was burning, she opened the door to the room. It was pitch black inside but soon the warm light of the lamp filled the space, revealing more of the same fine crafted furniture and a four-poster bed, covered with rich lines of embroidery.

Brandin looked around while Ilsa prepared the room for his use. Other than her soft motions, there was not another sound. The unrest in the city streets beyond the citadel walls might have been happening a thousand miles away. Sitting down on a small couch just opposite the bed, he thought of the beast. He had no idea who or what Oracandus was, but he had committed to ending his oppression. That fact made Brandin feel better than he had in months.

"You seem pleased with yourself, Stormborn." Ilsa's voice had taken on a deeper tone. When he looked up, she was staring at him, her eyes wide, a familiar smile twisting her thin lips. She twisted the ends of her braided hair around the fingers of her right hand.

Brandin jumped up, his hands balled into fists. "Damn you, angeli. What now? Haven't you done enough in Ravenhold? People are getting hurt in the streets, fires are burning throughout, and you stand there, abusing that poor woman's body with your grimy presence, smiling like the fool you are."

Isla shook her head slowly, her smile broadening. "No, no, no. You're wrong, Stormborn. All has gone according to plan."

"What do you mean," demanded Brandin.

The same laughter he had heard from the angeli, now coming through Ilsa's higher voice, sent shivers down Brandin's back. "No, no. I'm not telling. It's much more fun that way, don't you think?"

Brandin did not move. "So be it."

"Ah. There's no reason to pout. It is all for the greater glory of the gods, after all. Light a candle for Valdan. Say a prayer to the Stormbringer, your father."

"Leave, angeli. Let loose of the woman!"

The angeli, garbed in Ilsa's body, curtsied. "As you wish."

The woman's body drooped and her arms dropped to her sides. With her eyes closed, she seemed to be sleeping standing up. Brandin stood by and waited for her to wake. Her breathing was deep and regular. As he watched the rhythm changed, growing fainter until she let out a loud gasp. Ilsa's eyes opened.

"Oh dear. Forgive me. I must have dozed off." Her faced was flushed. "Do you need anything more this evening...my lord?" She said the last words awkwardly as though realizing who he was again, but not fast enough to interrupt her routine phrases.

Brandin shuddered but shook his head. "No. That is all. Thank you."

Ilsa curtsied and left him.

Though his weariness pressed him from every side, Brandin knew he would not sleep now. He sat on the couch, listening to the sound of his breathing, trying not to puzzle out the angeli's cryptic words, but failing. The creature seemed so arrogant, so sure of himself.

"Damn the gods and all of their plots upon mankind."

His voice sounded raw and weak. He'd come so far from his original course since leaving the Dragonsbane's decks. Brandin stared at the lamp, losing himself in the glow of the light.

"Tomorrow I face a monster," he whispered. "How did you get yourself into this, Stormborn. You're a bloody fool. That's what you are." Brandin shook his head. "Noble, but a fool playing at the hero again." His throat tightened. "I will do what I feel is right, father. I won't be caught up in the schemes of your kindred. When I finish, I will return to the swelling waves and the south-blowing winds and leave Belandria and Brandell Shay behind. I swear it by my own name and not by yours or any other god's."

10

Call to Arms

The skies above Ravenhold were clear blue. The birds flew about the parapets and ramparts of the citadels and other buildings surrounding it. The image was spoiled by the oily black plumes of smoke that cut through the clean blue field at different points throughout the city. Word had come that the riots were ended and the mobs disbanded. The work had shifted to getting the fires under control. Brandin received word of these events soon after waking, still in his clothes and draped across the couch. He mourned the loss of a night in the fine bed but soon busied himself with waking.

Isla knocked at the door and was soon bearing in a tray laden with eggs, bacon, and crusty bread. A flagon of fresh milk completed the repast. "Your breakfast, my lord."

Brandin smelled the smoked aroma of the bacon and his mouth watered. "Thank you, Ilsa."

Once the servant was gone, Brandin ate very slowly, savoring every morsel. He was smiling when Kreves came to call. The captain of the guards was dressed in a leather tunic that bore the marks of the armor he wore atop it. It was well worn. He nodded at the tray. "Good. Glad you're eating. It's been a busy morning so far. I've been busy with preparations. The men were chosen from among Lord Dungray's best soldiers. He insisted." He looked more closely at Brandin. "Did you sleep well?"

Brandin scooped another forkful of eggs into his mouth. "Like a baby."

Kreves snorted. "Not likely. You look like you were dragged down the stairs by your hair."

Brandin waved away the concerned. "I got enough sleep to do the job that needs to be done, Kreves. Oracandus will no longer hold sway over Dungray and Natya will be free once more." The words were said evenly but he knew his tone was flat. He was resigned to the facts. He chased away doubt before it even had a chance to root itself.

Kreves looked at him but didn't say another word about it. "When you're finished you can join us down in the main hall. You remember it from yesterday?"

"Yes."

Brandin ate breakfast, enjoying every flavor, savoring the aromas. He had always focused so much on his surroundings, enjoying every sight, every sound, and smell. At times, Brandin wondered if his senses were somehow more sensitive than those of other people. Was such focus the purview of the gods, giving glimpses of the layers of the world?

He tried to chase the thoughts from his mind and think more about what he would encounter in the forests outside Ravenhold. There was no reason to think the dwelling place of Oracandus was somehow bewitched. None that Lord

Dungray had shared with him, that is. Once he had finished, Brandin inspected his clothes and appearance. A little rough around the edges but he'd been in worse shape in the past. He left his room in the Dungray apartments and walked the halls out and away from them, catching the eye of the occasional guard, but little else. He had free reign now. Perhaps, Dungray allowed it to show his good intentions. Brandin was sure what to think so he just paid attention to putting one foot in front of the other until he returned to the part of the citadel Kreves indicated.

Once he entered the vaulted ceilings he heard several voices engaged in discussions. When he found them, Brandin saw Kreves waiting with Lord Dungray and several of his guards. They were several yards away, down a short flight of stairs. Just as he was about to walk down them, Natya came from a smaller side corridor. Her retinue stood well back to give them privacy.

Natya's black hair was smooth and reflected the snatches of light that brushed across it. Her face was pale and soft but Brandin only saw the remains of the bruises and cuts. She was garbed in a richly embroidered gown, with pearls sewn throughout the bodice. The cut of the gown accentuated her womanly figure. She was stunning and Brandin found it hard not to stare. As though she realized he was looking, she smiled. It was like sunlight spilling over the horizon at dawn.

She came within a foot of Brandin and stared up at him. "I wanted to thank you for what you are about to do. And... and apologize for my behavior before."

"Natya, I don't fault you for reacting to the truth. I can only hope that by removing Oracandus I take a first step towards making amends for the wrongs I've done in Belandria."

Natya reached out and put her small hand on his chest. "Oh, you are. I thought all was lost. My fate seemed sealed to that creature." She stepped closer, putting the other hand up next to the first. She was looking steadily into his eyes.

Brandin's heart beat faster.

"Please. It is not right. I can't stand the thought of your people being terrorized." Brandin turned his head, gritting his teeth. "Damn the gods," he muttered.

Natya heard his curse and her eyes widened. Then there was something else in them. Concern? "Brandin," she asked. Her voice was so light a musical; it flowed like honey.

Brandin looked down at her, more a woman than the girl he took her for at first. Her eyes remained still fixed upon him, even as her chest heaved in the bodice. His mouth went dry but he cracked a smile to break the tension that building inside.

"I must go now. Your father and his men wait for me."

Natya stepped back slowly. Then she rushed forward and rose on her tiptoes to put a soft kiss on his cheek before moving back and letting him go. As he continued down the staircase, his face tingled and his nose was filled with her perfume. He was slightly overcome by the heady mixture but Kreves and Dungray were too distracted to notice.

"The west gate is blocked by debris and it will take several hours to remove it. We cannot go to Oracandus' den by that route. We will have to traverse the whole city and exit by the east gate."

"Seems like you need another gate in this place." Brandin joked to cover his disconcertment. He glanced up to where Natya stood watching them. In truth, she was looking only at Brandin, her eyes glistening with a warm light. Brandin cleared his throat to keep from choking.

"It would help us save time, truly it would," said Dungray. The man seemed almost buoyant, his burdens nearly at an end. He was almost agreeable. Not a shred of the bitterness or anger for Brandell Shay. *All he sees now is Brandin Stormborn and his child's salvation*, thought Brandin.

Kreves was adjusting his leather gloves. He looked at Brandin. "You ready?"

Brandin nodded. "As I'll ever be."

"Good. Lord Dungray has given you a horse and you choose a weapon from his armory and whatever implements you might need to put down the beast."

"Thank you, Lord Dungray," said Brandin. He held out his hand and Dungray grabbed it in a firm grip.

"Be wary of Oracandus. He is a shrewd creature and viciously strong when he needs to be."

Brandin considered that. "Then I'll just have to outwit him."

Lord Dungray brushed a hand through his hair. He wore a pale blue coat and gray cloak that was lined with wolf hide. He was every inch the grizzled soldier himself. He was no fool, Brandin realized. *But maybe I am though*. Brandin wanted to smile but kept his face smooth.

"Let's get moving," said Kreves.

There were no more words exchanged. Brandin followed as Kreves moved through the long halls, saluting to men as he passed them. They entered a different area of the citadel and soon Brandin caught a whiff of horses. They were going directly to the stables. Just as they reached them, Kreves turned and they entered another hall, swarming with soldiers in the leather jerkins and silver armor, many in various states of dress. There was the clang of swords echoing from spaces unseen. Brandin realized they were heading to the armory first.

The way included many twists and turns to confuse invaders and to give the defenders time to mount defenses and keep them back from the weapons. Brandin found himself counting the turns and marking signs in case he became separated from Kreves. He had a feeling if he did, it would take hours to find his way out. Still, the rings of blades carried throughout the whole section, echoing off the walls and ceilings, reverberating back and forth adding layers to the clamor until he couldn't be sure of the direction of the source.

Kreves glanced back, squinting in the torches that barely relieved the deep gloom.

"It's not much longer."

"You know I don't need a weapon, don't you?"

Kreves bobbed his head. "Sure I do. I mean we all saw what you did out in the grasslands. But I have no idea what this creature is like. You might need every advantage we can give you."

Brandin had nothing to say to that so he followed Kreves the rest of the way far less nervous. They came to the armory rather abruptly. Around a corner stood, a thick iron gate that rose to the ceiling with a smaller door set in the middle. Six guards surrounded the door. One of them saluted Kreves.

"At ease. Open the gate. We need access to the armory."

"Right away, Captain."

The men jumped into action, removing the locks that secured the door on both ends, pulling free the heavy brace with a loud scraping that made Brandin wince. When it was free, the door came open easily. It had been well oils so it made barely a sound. One of the guards retrieved a torch and led them through the opening. Kreves and Brandin waiting just inside while the guard lit several of the torches in turn so that a golden light filled the stone room. Rows of spears, shields, swords, full armor, jerkins, axes, and other tools of defense filled the armory from one end to the other.

Brandin looked around to see if anything stood out. Meanwhile, Kreves picked out another sword and a new shield. While looking at several good, serviceable swords, Brandin glanced over at the wall and saw a spear that caught his eye. It was larger than the rest surrounding it. There was something about the haft, the shine of the metal in the torchlight that entranced him. He walked up to it and grasped the spear. He pulled it off the wall and the balance was just right. There was great age attached to the weapon. Squinting down at its length he saw the same characters that adorned the walls etched in the steel and along the leather-wrapped handle.

"Stormborn, you've picked up the *God's Finger*."

Brandin frowned down at the spear. "The what?"

Kreves came up to him, examining the oversized spear. "The God's Finger. That's what the spear is called. No body's been able to heave that thing around for more than a few seconds. Now you come in here and pick it up like it's nothing."

Brandin held the spear aloft in one hand, feeling the way the weight of it shifted as he twisted his wrist. "It's probably the finest spear I've ever carried," he admitted. "The balance and craftsmanship are exquisite." He shook his head and sniffed. "I suppose I shouldn't be surprised to find a weapon like this in this ancient place. Gods, Kreves, what else is down here?"

Kreves shrugged his shoulders. "Damned if I know everything. There's lots of old weapons tucked away down here. Just keep looking."

Brandin did.

The soldiers gasped when he emerged from the armory with the spear. They also gave him wide berth as though expecting him to start wreaking havoc there and then. The word was spreading about who he truly was. The fact frustrated him and likely confused many others. If word was reaching the people on the streets, that confusion would be greater. Crowds that had only recently caused damage through Ravenhold because of Brandell Shay were not prepared at all for the arrival of a starchild in their midst. As he made his way back out with Kreves, turning towards the stables now, he heard his name on many lips, servants and soldiers alike.

Brandin held the spear vertical, more like a staff than the weapon it was. Kreves glanced back occasionally. The man was smiling again like a bloody fool and there was nothing he could do to get him to stop. Brandin sighed at the unreasonableness of it all. He turned his attention to their passage to the halls. The smell of horses was stronger now and he could hear their noises now and a different sort of clanging issuing from the smithy.

Soon a line of the curious was trailing along after them. The God's Finger had that effect on people. Kreves did not stop until they had reached the tall doors that led to a yard open to the sky. Bright morning light poured in making Brandin clamp his eyes nearly shut until they adjusted to the light. Outside, the air was cool and refreshing after the citadel. He saw the plumps of smoke still rising into the sky but kept his mind to the task.

No more self-pity, he thought.

A cluster of horses was waiting, tethered to iron posts. A squad of Dungray's soldiers was standing by as well. Dungray was there too. The noble wore a long, flowing cloak so that it draped over his clothes. Brandin nodded greeting.

"It is time to bring this to an end, eh Stormborn."

Dungray smiled.

Brandin frowned. *No. It couldn't be. Not again so soon. Not him.*

"Yes, Lord Dungray. Oracandus will no longer be able to threaten Ravenhold. I promise you that."

Dungray pressed his palms together. "That is good, Stormborn. I am grateful." He almost smirked but recovered.

Anger coursed through Brandin but he resisted the urge to shout. The angeli was possessing Dungray. He didn't know why but he would not be goaded again.

"You are welcome, my lord." He strained to keep his voice even.

Brandin exchanged a look with Kreves. The other man arched his eyebrow quizzically, mouthing 'what.' Brandin whispered. "Later."

Kreves nodded and turned to the soldiers. "To arms, lads. You've been chosen to serve Lord Dungray on an important mission." While he spoke, Brandin went to the horse set aside for him, shifting the spear in his hands so he could get in the saddle. Kreves turned and pointed at him. "We have Brandin Stormborn in our midst. We shall prevail!"

A cheer rose up among them. Praises were given to Valdan the Stormbringer.

Brandin wanted to smack Kreves in the head but busied himself with adjusting his seat on the stallion instead. He used a leather cord to fix the God's Finger to the saddle above the satchels and waited. He looked again at Lord Dungray. He was smirking openly stopping to nod at Brandin. The next moment his head drooped. He slumped down, nearly falling before he regained his footing. Dungray blinked and looked around clearly confused. He spoke to a servant standing near-by who pointed at Brandin and the others.

Dungray walked up to Brandin. "Something happened to me just now that I do not know how to explain. I fear Oracan-dus might know what you intend."

"My lord, I will do what must be done." He met the no-ble's eyes. He was truly himself again. "Rest. Pray if you've the inclination, but remember our terms. Be kind to Natya. She still loves you though she might have trouble expressing it right now. She will forgive you, I think."

Dungray nodded. "Yes. Maybe you are right." As he walked away, Brandin turned his eyes to the heavens. Storm clouds were starting to move in. The smell of a coming rain permeated the air. He looked back towards the doors and saw Natya standing there. She just watched him. Brandin waved and she returned. Wheeling the horse around, he rode up to Kreves who was astride his brown steed.

"Let's get moving," Brandin said firmly. "I do not know what will be waiting for us in the forest."

Kreves kept silent but gave him a significant look. He turned to the other soldiers and issued orders. In a short time, they were riding out through the doors of the citadel and wind-ing through the streets towards the east gate.

An ominous rumble of thunder echoed across the skies.

11

Word from a God

Once they were beyond the city walls, the soldiers formed up single file and followed the road east then angled south around Ravenhold. Kreves and Brandin rode at the head of the line. At that hour, there was little traffic to speak of so they made decent time. The forest, situated as it was on the opposite side of the city, meant they would have to travel for a few hours on the trade roads, and only cutting off onto secondary trails when they were directly south of the city. The path was one of farmland and spare woodlands until they reached the dense growth forests on the west.

The skies were soon choked with thick, gray clouds. The rumbling of thunder continued throughout the journey but so far they saw no traces of lightning. No rain fell. The storm was slow in building. Brandin found comfort in the sound and thought he could smell the ocean on the gusts that periodically blew against them on the road. As they continued along the road, those that dwelled on the farms and other home places became curious, came out, and watched them ride past. Children pointed and gaped at the men riding in burnished silver armor. A few shouted about the yellow-haired man with the spear strapped to his saddle. Brandin waved to some but mostly he brooded on what was on the trail. Oracandus was out there somewhere. Though they had an idea where he dwelled, Brandin felt certain he would see them long before they saw him. Whatever sort of creature he was, he was probably dangerous and unpredictable.

"I could use a drink of wine."

Kreves, riding next to him now, smiled. "Sorry, Stormborn, only water in the skins. We'll have a drink once we've dealt with Oracandus."

Brandin grudgingly had to admire Kreves's faith. That is what it was. Faith. He had faith in him. He believed that he would prevail. Maybe that bothered Brandin more than anything else. He wasn't one of the gods and had no desire to be treated as such.

They rode at an easy pace, not wanting to tire the horses in case they needed to run at a moment's notice. Everyone grew wary as they continued on the road first south then gradually west as it angled around Ravenhold. The farmlands gave way to emptier grasslands, though not like the Black Grass they crossed the previous day. Brandin had no interest in fighting off another pack of zeranths. More peddler wagons and farmers were moving their produce to the markets in rickety carts on the road than might have been normal for the time of day but it seemed quiet. He scanned the clumps of trees that sometimes marked boundaries between on homestead and another or which provided screens to keep the winds from blowing away topsoil. The air was cooler with the breezes

gusting continually. Above them, the storm clouds continued to churn and roil but there was still no rain. The thunder
rumbled and from time to time, they saw a bolt of lightning
strike in the middle of faraway fields. The soldiers, burdened
by their armor spoke in short snatches but otherwise tried
to keep their attention on those lightning strikes. The bolts
could strike them, clustered as they were, but Brandin wasn't
too concerned yet. If the storm progressed anymore, they
would have to stop and seek shelter in one of the barns or
houses they saw on the road.

The party rode on, Brandin in the lead, until they spot-
ted the trail that diverged from the main trade road. They
were directly south of the city they would take the shortcut
to reduce how much time it would take to reach the western
road. Even from so far away, they could see the forests on the
western horizon, smudged and indistinct behind a curtain of
mist that was curling around the boughs and down to the
trunks. The land surrounding the trail was more tall grass
with some thickets of thin, wispy trees. Beneath the sparse
canopies, grew all manner of bush and bramble. The trail cut
through the tangle of undergrowth but only amounted to a
narrow band of bare ground. Brandin and the others were
forced to ride single file again to avoid scratches and scrapes
from the leathery vines and thorns.

Once they were inside the path, the density of the growth
obscured much of the way ahead. Brandin considered turning back and returning to the trade road since it was more
open with some of the encroaching grass and trees cut back
from the edges. As it was, they might stumble upon Oracandus with little notice whatsoever. Through the trees, he saw
the sun was halfway to its zenith. *Probably four hours on the*

road, he thought. *At this rate, we won't get through to the western road until after midday.*

Brandin did not try to hurry them though. The Kreves and the soldiers kept their pace with him and maintained vigilance in case they were ambushed. After a few more hours, they reached a relatively clear space in the tangle where the trees largely fell away leaving patches of shrubs and bramble bushes and the tall grass. Atop the horses, Brandin could again see a bit of the western forests.

He looked back at the soldiers and held up a fist. Kreves understood the signal and raised his voice. "We'll rest here for a few minutes. Water the horses and stretch your legs."

Brandin slid from the saddle and walked away from the others keeping to the trail and listening to the rustlings surrounding. He took a sip from his canteen, having pulled it from the saddle on the way down. The water was starting to warm but was still fresh. He sighed thinking of wine. Another breeze rushed through the clearing rustling the grass so that it seemed to whisper and shaking the bushes so they swayed. Again, the scent of the open seas came to him. He sucked in the comforting smell. At that moment, a deep growling thunder rolled across the skies just above them. No lightning just the protracted rumble. The horses were skittish and a few were trying to shake loose.

Brandin looked all around them, frowning. *Why do I smell the sea so far from the coast? What devilry is at work?*

The clouds, black and angry looking, gathered above them, swirling around. Then came lightning, forking across the skies so that grotesque shapes took form in the surfaces of the clouds. Brandin stared at them. The thunder boomed and one of the horses tore away and bolted back down the

114

trail. He heard Kreves curse. "Don't, Wilkes. Stay here. No use wasting time chasing after the damned horse."

Kreves turned around, gazing at the ominous skies, then looked at Brandin. There were no answers for what was happening. He just waited there well away from the others. The center of the spiral moved until it was directly over his position. Again, the smell of the ocean wafted in the air and he though he could hear the pounding of the waves against the coastline. Looking at the others, he had the distinct feeling they were not sharing his experience. A suspicion bloomed in his mind. Brandin gritted his teeth and resisted the idea.

"No. It can't be," he muttered. "Why here? Why now?"

A mist, like he saw wreathing the forests to the west, slipped into the clearing, creeping up through the shrubs and brambles, and turning the Kreves and the soldiers to shadows.

"Stormborn," called Kreves. "Are you still there?"

"I am."

The mists encircled him but remained well away from him so that he was sealed inside. The mists thickened to a true fog that became so white he could see nothing but a few shadowy clumps of grass and the nearest shrubs. Directly above, the skies continued to churn. The wind changed course and grew stronger, now moving as a spiral around him. After a moment, he was straining to stay upright. The winds howled, thunder boomed every few seconds as it accompanied streaks of lightning. Another roar sounded in the fog. As he gasped, an enormous flash of lightning struck down in the clearing. He was knocked flat and skidded across the grass to the edge of the fog wall. His sight was blurry but he saw something—no someone—emerging from the white-hot glow.

The figure of a man emerged, at first seeming like he was made of fog. The man towered over him by at least twenty feet. Brandin did not move but stared steadily at the figure. Wind still roared and his ears were popping and cracking painfully. The man took a step towards him and seemed to shrink with each step until he was normal height. He was broad-shouldered with long blond hair bound in intricate braids. He wore a small beard and earrings decorated both ears. His eyes were pale blue. The man was dressed in a richly embroidered tunic the color of the sky and darker green legging he wore tucked into boots studded with silver. At his hip, he wore a sword shaped like a lightning bolt. About the man, there was a slight glow.

Brandin started to move. He winced and rubbed at his back where he must have struck a root or half-buried rock. The man took a step forward.

"Are you hurt?" The man's voice was deep, reminding Brandin of thunder.

Brandin sat up and then got to his feet, brushing his hands on his pants. "Not really. A few bruises. Nothing more."

The man nodded. "You must be wondering who I am?"

Brandin did not blink but stared at the man. "You're my father. You are Valdan the Stormbringer."

Valdan nodded. "Yes. So you do know. I have wanted to speak to you for some time now. But there were complications."

"Complications?" Brandin felt heat rising to his face. "What sort of complications? I have lived my whole life knowing that I was the son of a god but never having a father. What sort of complications kept you away all of these years?"

Valdan bowed his head. "The will of the gods."

"But you're a god. Who do you answer to? You make the ways and the means. You're the Stormbringer. You tell the winds where to blow and send down thunder and lightning upon the seas bringing storms to the world of men. You could have answered. So many times I prayed as a boy for an answer, anything to let me know you cared. But there was nothing."

"I do care, Brandin."

Brandin shook his head. "Why are you here? This cannot be a coincidence. I have been harried by the angeli since I stepped foot in this realm."

"He was directed to turn you from your course, my son."

"That was my decision. I will not be guided by the gods. Do you mean to turn me from this path as well? Am I not meant to destroy the beast, Oracandus?"

Valdan eyes were like storm clouds. "Yes."

"This is about more than the life of one noblewoman or even one city, isn't it?"

"Yes, it is."

"Is this why you decided to come down here?"

Valdan walked towards him. The winds that swirled them seemed to abate and the lightning let up so that it came less frequently. "In part. As I said, I long wanted to come to you, but there were matters that kept me from doing so. The will of my brothers and sisters made it almost impossible for me to act before now."

Brandin tried to make sense of his father's words. "You were forbidden to come? The gods can stop one another from acting?"

Valdan nodded. "When it comes to certain matters, yes.

The fate of our children is one area where it has been decreed that we have little involvement. The lives of our Stars are meant to shine brighter than others and provide guidance to the rest of mankind, but not so much that they worship them rather than us."

"Strange politics, father."

Valdan smiled--a beautiful thing that lit the god's face. "Yes. Strange and terrible. I do not expect forgiveness, Brandin. I only want to let you know that I truly had no choice. You have followed your own course as you should, in most things. The only frustration felt by our family is that you've rejected them utterly. It has made you unpopular among the starborn."

Brandin barked a laugh. "Good. I'm glad I've made my point."

Valdan nodded gravely. "Yes, but at a terrible cost. More than once, I'm afraid. Still, there are those among my brethren who stand by and let you do what you think is best without stepping in and twisting events in order to punish one they see as a blasphemer."

Brandin's throat grew tight and he had trouble speaking. "You mean..." He let the words trail off.

"The revolts in this kingdom spiraled out of control because the gods decided to teach you a lesson. Only just lately, they have used the angeli to move you." Valdan held out his hands. "You cannot thwart the will of the gods forever. You have a responsibility as one of our children to serve and do good works so mankind is pointed to the heavenly lights."

"What if I still refuse?"

Valdan spread his hands before him.

Brandin snorted. "There will be consequences."

"Is there nothing you can do? You are one of them. How might your will be done, father? Do I have to obey all the gods or might I choose whom I might serve?"

Valdan held a finger to his lips. "Such questions are best left unspoken for now, but they are important, I assure you. If you will come to me and speak them in the days ahead I will try to answer. First, remove Oracandus. He threatens many people and many interests among the realms of men."

"Is this all the answers you can offer me? I have questions, father. Many questions."

"In time, my son. Be patient. I will answer them." Valdan began to glow as though the sun was trying to burst forth from his heart. He smiled. "It is good to look upon you and speak with you, Brandin. Your mother has raised you well. You've accomplished much for the greater good. I am proud of you. I must go but we shall meet again."

Brandin's chest pounded with panic. "No, wait. Don't leave yet!"

"Goodbye, Brandin, son of storms. You have my blessings and power." Valdan gestured beyond the veil of fog. "You found the spear I left for you. Use it well."

The winds dropped away and the clouds melted away so that the midday sky was revealed. In moments, Brandin could see the rest of the trail come into view. The soldiers were clustered together, waiting. Kreves was astride his horse. When he saw Brandin he waved.

"You're alive! Thanks be to the gods!"

Brandin waved back and walked back to where they waited. The soldiers, though seasoned veterans, goggled at him. Their surprise was evident. The horses shied away from him and they parted so he could reach his mount. The spear was there, shining in the sunlight streaming into the clearing. The storm was gone. The heavy clouds were dissipating to wisps of gray to be burned away in the sun's glow.

Kreves rode up beside him, looking down anxiously. "What happened? You just disappeared into that...that storm."

Brandin adjusted the bridle on the horse and checked the straps on the saddle. "We'll speak of it later. We need to make up for lost time."

Kreves looked down on Brandin for a few seconds more before wheeled his horse about to face the others. "Mount up, lads."

Though a few were hesitant at first, in the end, everyone was ready to ride after a few moments. The presence of the sun was welcome. As they continued down the trail, Brandin sniffed for even a trace of the sea but found nothing but the smells of the trees and the grass.

In due time, the party of riders came to the western trade road and set off out in the open at a trot. The dark band of the woods was directly in front of them now, still wreathed in mist. Brandin reached down to run his fingers across the handle of the spear. He felt strong and was ready for whatever Oracandus would try. As they rode ever closer to the edge of the forest, he kept the image of his father foremost in his mind. Many feelings warred in his mind and heart, but he welcomed them. What mattered most was that he had not been willingly abandoned to his fate. There were reasons to believe otherwise. He would get his answers from the Stormbringer. The realization brought relief so deep that all of his other bitterness began to crack.

"Thank you, father." He heeled the stallion and set him to a gallop. Kreves and the others set out after him.

12

Shadows in the Forest

Brandin halted the others on the edge of the forest for a hasty lunch. All of them would be more effective with a full belly. The pause gave him more time to reflect on the conversation with his father. The more he thought about it the more it all seemed more a dream than a meeting in the waking world. He had cultivated his animosity for the gods based mostly on the teaching and beliefs spouted by the priests and temple servants in the realms he had visited during his travels. While Brandin had encountered various creatures that were known only in myths and legends, he had never faced one of the gods themselves. The meeting with Valdan confirmed the deeper, innate understanding he had about his parentage. Words spoken by his mother in rare moments took on new meanings.

"I want those answers, father."

He ripped into his bread and ate a hunk of cheese the size of his fist to go with it. Then he washed the dry meal down with more water. Before heading into the murky wilderness, the soldiers replenished the water they carried with them in a small stream that wound parallel to the road, which in turn ran parallel to the forest itself. Only a rougher stretch of road entered the forest. This older trail used to be a main thoroughfare in ancient days. Brandin listened to Kreves ramble about the history and the reason for the redirection of the trade roads.

The forests had been a draw for bandits, outlaws, and other sordid villains over the years. Some of the rebels who had been involved in the Casteny Revolt were rumored to have sought refuge in the dense growth where darkness ruled more often than not. It was no wonder that Oracandus was drawn to the forest. The reputation of the place probably suited his kind.

Brandin mounted up first, patting the stallion's head and whispering soothing words into his ears. "Let's ride. We have to get inside before it gets much later. Use as much sunlight as we can get trying to box him in."

Kreves adjusted his gloves before mounting his horse. "From what I've learned, Oracandus keeps to a certain part of the forest. It's near a larger stream--possibly the one that feeds that little trickle." He pointed back to the streamlet. "Stormborn, perhaps we should split up so he doesn't get any ideas about moving deeper into the forest. If he does that, we'd have no way of keeping up with him. The horses will have less room to move around and the ground likely slopes a bit once you get about five miles further west." He pointed again but to show him the upward curve of the tree line.

Brandin nodded. "Split them up evenly and have them head northward next to the tree line for half a mile. Then they can come in and help us close the net. The only thing

Oracandus will be able to do is come out closer to the edge of the forest where the trees aren't so densely packed and we can have more of an advantage."

"It's sound good in theory," replied Kreves. "But what if he does something else. This is no dumb beast. He changed his shape and might be able to hide further. He could sneak up on us unawares and strike before any of us could raise a spear or sword against him."

Brandin conceded that fact. "You may be right. What do you suggest?"

"I know where that stream flows. Let's ride directly for it, staying together, but splitting into two halves so that one is on each bank of the stream. We'll lead the horses along if we can't ride. There is a fork in that stream. I remember it from my childhood. He'll likely be holed up somewhere in the rocks or crevasses at that point in the stream's course. There are plenty of hiding places where Oracandus can avoid detection if we aren't careful."

"Then we will have to be careful."

Kreves nodded. "Yes."

"Take the lead. You know this area, Kreves. You and your men have the advantage in that sense." Brandin rode up and leaned closer. "When it comes to confronting him, I will come out first with this spear in hand to skewer Oracandus before he can mount a better defense."

Kreves considered his words. "You mean to face him alone?"

"I think that is the best way. It keeps your men out of danger."

Kreves huffed. "We're not cowards, Brandin Stormborn. We are ready to serve Belandria until our last breaths."

Brandin put his hand on Kreves's shoulder, trying to placate his friend's injured pride. "I know the extent of your devotion. But if we can limit the bloodshed this day, won't that be a far better outcome?"

Kreves shifted in the saddle, then he glanced into Brandin's eyes. "Perhaps, that is true. I am ready to face death but only if I absolutely have to do it. I certainly do not court it like some berserker."

"Good. You're not a complete fool then."

Kreves opened his mouth to protest then smirks. "It seems not."

The soldiers were all ready. Brandin exchanged a few words with the other officers since some of them would lead half of their party to the opposite side of the stream before commencing inwards, following the course upstream. Once the instructions were given, the men saluted Kreves and Brandin in turn and rode off. Their silver armor reflected the afternoon sun. The remaining soldiers sat astride their horses, ready to ride with them. Kreves chose to follow the old road in first and then break off for the stream at a point familiar to him. They entered the forest and cut through the mists. From the moment they entered the forest, it was as though evening had descended early. Shadows appeared in the boughs and the sounds of the animals were muted like they were holding their breath. Brandin had no notions of Oracandus' appetites. No doubt he ate just about anything he could catch, including soldiers. The thought wasn't very pleasant. His hand drifted again to the haft of the spear and then loosened the ties that bound it fast to his saddle.

"Be ready." He spoke softly.

Kreves passed the word down the line of soldiers. The

jangling of bridles and the twinkling of their plate armor sounded much louder in the stillness of the woods. The horses were moved slowly and cautiously on the crumbling remnants of stone. The men held crossbows and spears alike, ready to let loose at the first sign of trouble. Brandin went ahead and pulled God's Finger out and held it by the haft. He listened, keeping his breath slow and even. His eyes scanned the lighter patches between the thick, dark trunks of the trees so he would have a better chance of tracking any movements.

Kreves rode just a few paces ahead, moving his head back and forth, speaking softly to himself. Brandin though he might be praying but then wondered to which god he prayed. This made him tighten his grip on the spear and refocus on the forest shadows. They rode like this for some time before Brandin caught the first bubbling sounds of running water. He dismounted and tied the stallion to a tree. Ahead, Kreves had already taken to the ground but trailed his horse behind him, taking slow deliberate steps until he stopped to secure his horse to another tree branch. He waited until Brandin joined him.

"There's the stream below." He pointed at the narrow ribbon of water coursing at the base of a rocky ravine."

"It's spring-fed, isn't it?"

Kreves smiled. "Right. It comes out of the ground further west of the split. The ground is mostly rock up that way. The ravine grows steeper and there are many places where Oracandus can hide. I played in the shallow caves many times during the summer." Kreves frowned now. "This placed seem so much brighter then."

Brandin stared around at the gnarled trees that seemed to grow so close together that they formed a sort of dome over them. The stream was much louder owing to the way the shape of the land amplified noises. The stones that formed part of the banks below was covered in thick, green moss and small yellow flowers grew at points along the water's edge. He noticed that the hillside was not even. There were two rows of flat paths that zigzagged downward.

"Looks like ramps," said Brandin.

"I think there were a series of buildings around here. It might have been a settlement at one time. Not much in the way of ruins now, eh?"

Brandin agreed. The sound of rocks sliding brought him back to the present. His eyes darted up the hill and back down again. He gestured to Kreves, pointing towards a tall rock that jutted up out of the ground. There was a ring of trees surrounding it, creating a natural fence. The perfect place for someone to hide, Brandin thought.

He started down the hillside. Two of the Ravenhold soldiers followed after him, making surprisingly little noise in their armor. Brandin made it down to the stream bank without any mishaps. The area surrounding them was silent. After several minutes, Kreves and the rest of the men were down.

"We checked uphill, but I saw nothing. Not one sign."

"Maybe it was nothing," said Brandin.

A deep, guttural cry pierced the stillness of the forest above them. The crash of branches breaking and leaves brushing against each other was followed by the appearance of something falling, a living shadow that hurtled towards him. The other soldiers screamed. Brandin was struck hard without even the chance to bring up his spear to ward off the blow. There was a blur of motion as the shadow sailed in the air, landing on the higher ground amidst the trees and rocks.

He was gone by the time Brandin regained his wits.

"Gods, was that him?"

Kreves came to his side. "I do believe it was. Are you hurt?"

Brandin was searching every corner of the forest directly surrounding them, looking in the shadows twice, ears pitched towards every sound.

"Not really. How are the men?"

Kreves took an assessment of the soldiers. "No one was touched but you."

"Stay alert," said Brandin.

"You don't have to worry about that, I think." Kreves glanced at the soldiers. They were searching the shadows above them, crossbows set and ready to fire. They wouldn't be caught unawares again. Oracandus would look like a pincushion.

"Let move towards the fork in the stream. Have two men stay back with the horses."

Brandin picked up the spear and started west along the bank. The rock was slippery in places, but he made good time. The men, encumbered by their armor moved somewhat slower but remained remarkably quiet. They followed the course of the stream without any other attacks. Still, Brandin believed Oracandus was watching them. Watching and waiting for another chance to surprise them. There were just too many shadows to hide in. Beneath the thick canopies of the trees, they were riding in an early twilight. Brandin considered lighting torches but doing so would take too much time.

The forest was still again. The small rustlings of hares and squirrels came less frequently until they stopped completely. The soldiers walked in pairs, keeping watch for their prey just as much as they kept looking for the other soldiers who had split off to approach on the opposite bank. Sometime in the afternoon—at least, Brandin thought it was the afternoon—Kreves waved at him from several paces up the path.

"I see the fork up ahead. We're almost there."

"Good. See anything like a campsite?"

Kreves squinted. "Nothing yet. Remember," he said. "He probably holed up in one of the crevasses or small caves up around the wedged rocks. We won't find much without poking our noses into them."

Brandin smiled. "Sounds like fun, eh Kreves?"

"Right, loads of fun, Stormborn. Like hunting a cave bear only Oracandus is smarter and probably has sharper teeth."

After a few hundred paces more, they stopped to rest in a small clear covered with broken trees and huge slabs of stone that formed a natural roof. Within it, Kreves found the first signs that someone had occupied the space recently. Brandin sniffed the air and caught the scent of something but couldn't be sure what it was.

"What is that smell?"

Kreves wrinkled up his nose. "Smells like deer piss."

"Ah," said Brandin. He had spent far more time at sea than he ever had in the forests and fields beyond the shore. He was quite out of his element. "You think he was here too though. Maybe trying to hide any signs of habitation using the deer?"

Kreves knelt near the ground and picked through the fallen leaves and twigs. He smelled pieces of the brush. "I don't smell anything else in here. It doesn't mean Oracandus hasn't been here. The site makes sense. Good shelter and he could keep mostly dry and use the brush here to keep warm without lighting a fire."

Brandin sat down on a rock, propping the spear against him. The other soldiers entered the shelter but Kreves had three of them take up posts to watch for the others. For a while, no one spoke but all were listening to the forests around them. The shadows deepened as the daylight faded. Afternoon slipped into early evening.

"We'll set up a camp here," said Kreves. "We'll gather up some of this brush to burn before it's too dark to see."

"With any luck, the rest of the men will show up here before darkness falls." Brandin squinted just to see more than a few hundred paces into the growing murk. "They'd better hurry. Probably not a good idea to get caught out there with no fire to light the way."

Kreves agreed and walked out to the edge of the shelter. "Grasley, Orthel, once we've lit a fire, I want to take a couple of those branches and set up torches just outside. By the gods' luck, they will see them as a beacon and make it in." He added, "We can only hope the lads we left with the horses had the sense to light fires too. Maybe Oracandus will avoid them."

As darkness fell, the forests awoke and soon a host of cries, hoots, and gibbers filled up the silence. A simple stew was made from bits of dried vegetables and meat taken from satchels. The soldiers in armor removed the silver plates and everyone gathered closer to the blaze. Brandin sighed contentedly as the heat poured into his weary bones. The night air was much cooler now. The crackling of the dried logs was quite loud too. Everyone was taking turns at guarding the parameter of the camp. After another couple of hours, Brandin took his turn using the haft of his spear like a walking stick to climb atop a mound of dirt a few paces from where the others dozed.

The darkness was complete. Brandin faced the black forest so his night vision wasn't diminished by torchlight. He watched and listened, straining to hear past the natural rustlings of the forest's denizens, but mindful that Oracandus was out there spying on them. He wanted to call the beast out to see if he was enough of a man to face him. He had hoped to have a better sense of what he was like but that would have to wait until dawn. Part of Brandin was tempted to go hunting him on his own, unencumbered by the others in their armor. He could be much quieter in the forests than the others. At least he thought he could.

He heard a twig snap somewhere to his right. Brandin brought up the spear and took a few steps, trying to keep his footing on the unseen ground. "Damn this darkness. Not even the moon to light the way."

Something was moving through the underbrush in the same general area.

"Who goes there?" He said the words loudly and clearly.

There was no reply.

Brandin raised his voice again. "Who is out there? Answer me. Show yourselves."

More sounds of leaves rustling, twigs breaking, as someone or something pushed through the shadows.

He felt his body tensing, anxious and the blood was flowing through his veins and his chest throbbed. His grip on the spear was tight. He tried to loosen it so his fingers wouldn't numb. He advanced a few steps more into the forest. The light of the camp was at his back. He could see very little. His ears were his only guides now.

Someone was dragging their feet through the brush and fallen leaves. Whoever it was, wasn't attempting stealth.

"Last warning," Brandin called. "Who is out there?"

"Please," a voiced called out, very weakly. "Please wait. We're unarmed."

"I'm Brandin Stormborn. Who is out there?"

"Commander Barring and one of my men."

"You're from the other party?"

"Yes," said Barring. "We were attacked by the beast. Rills and I were the only ones to survive."

"Damn the gods," Brandin growled. He pitched his voice for them to hear him. "Do you see the torches?"

"Yes, Stormborn," said Barring.

"Follow them in. We're camped down here beneath a roof of trees and stone."

Brandin turned back and dashed towards the camp himself. Kreves stumbled to his feet when came into the light.

"What is it?"

Brandin pointed back the way he'd come. "Oracandus attacked the other half of your men. Only two made it back in. They're making their way down here now."

"Gods," gasped Kreves.

Brandin squeezed the haft of his spear until his knuckles ached. "I'm going to bury this blade in that bloody beast's chest. I swear this in the name of my father, Valdan the Storm bringer."

The soldiers were all wide awake now and staring at him. They saw what he didn't: A glow that seemed to surround the starchild in their midst and the fury carved in his face.

13

The Hunter Sees

Wane shafts of sunlight pierced the thick curtain of leaves to announce the coming dawn. Brandin had been awake well before the first glimmers of light fell to dispel the deep darkness surrounding their camp. He was sitting next to remains of the campfire, facing outward. The stream bubbled below them. He sipped hot tea from a chipped mug. Back behind him, Kreves cleared his throat as he tossed aside his blanket and sat up.

"Good morning, Stormborn," he said groggily.

"Morning to you, Kreves."

The sleeping forms of the other men, including Commander Barring who suffered injuries from Oracandus, were arrayed around the flames. Two other soldiers were already up and about, finishing out their turns at watch. The men approached with their cloaks wrapped tightly around them. The air was colder the further away one ventured from the fire.

"We need to get ready to move. I want to see if we can

pick up his trail. We have to start where the others were attacked."

Kreves's expression, muddled by sleep, turned grave. "I do not know how well Barring is to travel. We may have to leave him behind."

Brandin bowed his head. He couldn't ignore what was on his mind to do. He twisted around so he faced the fire. He looked at Kreves over the flames. "I am going after him myself."

Kreves frowned. "You'll never be able to find him in here. You've already admitted being a poor tracker."

Brandin got up, drawing the spear up with him. "I'll manage well enough. I have a feeling Oracandus will come to me."

"Still, I am going with you." Kreves' voice was firm. His eyes were alight with his determination.

The laughter poured from his throat before Brandin could choke it back. He let it roll out, letting the tension and fear flow with it. The unexpected sound roused the entire camp. The laughter stopped when tears leaked from the corners of his eyes. He wiped them away.

"So be it, my friend. Maybe you've earned that much. Though I do not want your death on my hands."

"I won't hand my life over so easily, Stormborn."

Across the fire, Commander Barring struggled to sit up. "Captain Kreves, sir, I will be ready to continue the pursuit."

"You need to save your strength, Commander. You will be in charge of the rest of the men. I want to move back east to where we left the horses. If the gods favor us at all the lads we left with them are still alive. You will set up camp and wait there for the next day. If we've not returned, then ride back to

Ravenhold. Are my orders clear?"

Barring wiped sweat from his forehead. "Yes, Captain."

"Good," said Kreves. He turned to Brandin. "I'm ready when you are. We are going hunting together, just you and I."

Kreves gathered supplies for them both and made sure he was well armed. He did not take any armor but chose to stay in his leather jerkin. The hide was tough enough to deflect blows and allow him to run if need be. Brandin wore no armor or protective garb. He wore a simple shirt and coat beneath his jacket. In packing, a couple of soldiers volunteered a knife or a package of dried beef for them. Brandin thanked the men for their contributions. After a light breakfast of bread and a couple of robin eggs, he and Kreves headed out. They moved away from the shelter of stone and the smells of the campfire and the voices of the men soon faded.

For nearly a quarter-hour Brandin hiked along the stream, just keeping a steady westward pace. Only then, did he stop and start listening to the forest. Kreves kept his eyes on their path, marking out familiar landmarks and keeping a tally of their progress in his mind.

Standing on the bank, so that the gurgling of the chill water was loud, Kreves stopped just a pace away. He spoke low. "How do you know we're going the right way?"

Brandin's eyes darted up into the shadowy boughs, scanning the patches of the forest floor revealed in the morning sunlight. "Call it a hunch."

"A hunch," said Kreves. "Now we're operating on blind faith?"

Brandin shook his head. "No, Kreves. I believe Oracandus is tracking us right now, maybe watching us. I also believe he was told I was coming for him. He will attack again, but this time I will be ready for him."

After saying it, Brandin felt a sliver of doubt. He didn't say so, but he wondered whether this Oracandus might finally be a match for him. The fears, the concerns, were all too human and felt wrong deep inside. The divine spark in him denied such weakness. He kept his inner struggle quiet and did his best to watch the forest more closely. Kreves was just a couple of paces back, sword in hand. He moved very deliberately through the undergrowth so that he made very little noise even on the brittle and dried leaves. Brandin did fine considering his lack of familiarity with hunting on dry land.

Get me a line and a hook and I could catch all manner of creatures from the sea, Brandin mused.

After a time, the banks of the stream grew steeper so Brandin and Kreves had to spend more time negotiating up the side of the ravine, which was growing steeper. Brandin used his spear to steady himself so he wouldn't tumble down to the rocky banks or into the chilling waters. The stream was deeper at that point, and according to Kreves, it would be deepest near the spring that drew the waters from far below the earth. The trees grew in tangled knots as they journey to the heart of the waters and there were far more rocks than green grass to be seen.

Brandin felt Oracandus' eyes on them like a prickly sensation on the back of his neck. He kept searching for him lurking behind the thick, rugged trunks of the maples, elms, and oaks that grew up in tight bunches wherever he looked. The whole surface of the forest was an uneven jumble of jagged hills between different branches of the ravine. The forest was moist and the smell of the earth, the moss, and dampened bark was pungent. Brandin could not smell much else and wondered if it helped Oracandus hide better.

"If we had a hound to hunt with, we could make far shorter work of him."

"Yes, true," said Kreves. "Unless the smell of beast scared him off."

"Have you noticed anything? Even a hint that Oracandus is out there?"

"No. Not a trace. I've been squinting in this half-light for so long I'm seeing spots."

"Time for another break. Isn't it about lunchtime?" Brandin spoke loudly.

Kreves looked at him and shrugged his shoulders. "I suppose it could be. More a feeling than really knowing where the sun is in the skies above this infernal mess." He gestured to above and around them.

In that place, it was closer to full darkness than twilight. Only a few faints sunbeams penetrated to the stony ground. They walked a few paces to where one of those lights shone faintly and sat down on the pitiful patch of leave-covered grass. Kreves pulled out his blanket roll and shook it out for them to sit on. Brandin was already drinking from his water pouch. At least, the stream had been a reliable source of water during the course of their journey. They had a luncheon of harder bread, the last of the apples Kreves had snagged from vendors in Ravenhold during their departure.

"Thanks," said Brandin as Kreves tossed him one of the wrinkled fruit.

"It's a privilege, Stormborn."

"Stormborn!"

A deep, growling voice cried his name like a curse. Brandin jerked at the sound and was up on his feet brandishing the spear. Kreves was a second behind him. He was held his blade poised to strike.

Then he came at them. Oracandus rushed them so fast, moving surely on the uneven ground, moving like a horse at full gallop. He headed straight for them, charging and screaming a sound that made Brandin's whole body tremble. Beside him, Kreves' eyes were so wide you could see the whites around his dark pupils.

"Stormborn," cried Oracandus. "Stormborn!"

Each time his name was shouted, it became part a cry of outrage part fear.

"I know you, Stormborn! I know your name, son of Stormbringer."

Oracandus collided with Brandin, driving him to the ground so hard he was dazed for a few seconds. In those moments, the creatures hoisted him in the air and threw him several feet away.

"No!" Kreves came at the creature with his sword moving so fast it was a blur.

When his eyes cleared Brandin watched Kreves keep Oracandus at bay with his blade, though it was clear that he was toying with his friend. Brandin gritted his teeth and ran towards them.

"Move, Kreves," Brandin screamed.

Kreves darted to one side, dropping low as Brandin jump over him and slammed into Oracandus. Hands locked together, he could smell and feel the creature's hot breath on his face. A face contorted in bestial rage, spittle leaking down a pointed chin. Oracandus' eyes were yellow like those of a wolf. They moved around in a circle, thrashing and shoving one another. Brandin felt the fullness of the creature's strength pressing back at him.

The next moment they tumbled down into the ravine, twisting end over end. Brandin let go of Oracandus to protect his head from the rocks but remained tangled up with him as they reached the bank of the stream. He was pulled free and came to rest on the slick stones. Oracandus tumbled into a wider point in the stream that formed a pool and sank below the surface.

The forest was still except for the gurgling water. Brandin got up, wincing from the scrapes and bruises that were spread across his body. He watched and waited for Oracandus to come at him again. Above him, he heard Kreves scrambled on the uneven ground, sending rocks and sticks tumbling down the side.

"You okay," he called down.

"I am. Be ready. He's hiding beneath the water."

Seconds passed and there was nothing. Not even bubbles to disturb the surface. Brandin retrieved the spear and walked along the bank, making his way across the wet rocks carefully.

"Do you see anything?" Kreves had made it halfway down before stopping.

Brandin listened to the current of water moving through the ravine. No splashing. Nothing to show Oracandus had emerged. *Surely he did not die so easily?*

The ground shook beneath him. Then it rose up so fast Brandin was forced to leap uphill, using his spear to secure himself. The slab of stone flew up and struck just a few paces away. Oracandus was there an instant later. He was on Brandin straining to reach his face. His pale face was contorted and dripping wet. Mud covered his body.

"I'm going to bite your head off, Stormborn."

Brandin held him back though his muscles strained painfully to hold back the weight of Oracandus. "How did you know I was coming for you?" Brandin grunted the question.

"I heard them speaking your name. You think I do not know of the children of my former masters? Do you think I am a fool? I know they sent you, starchild. Sent you to kill me they did!" Oracandus' voice rose in pitch until he was wailing."

"Yah! For Ravenhold!"

Kreves had reached them and struck Oracandus' with his sword. The blade bit into the flesh of his shoulder and back. The creature screamed in pain and flung himself back down the hill to the stream again. He did not sink in the water but stared back at them. He touched his wounds.

"You'll die for that, little man! I'll grind your bones between my jaws."

Brandin sat up. Kreves knelt beside him.

"What now?"

Brandin gaped. "Move!" Both men rolled out of the way.

Oracandus jumped again, sailing through the air below the trees. He growled and landed just where they had been. Brandin took up the spear and waved it before him. Though the creature tried to bat it out of his hands, he held on. He lashed out and managed a glancing cut on Oracandus' leg. More screams of outrage but he wasn't retreating now. Kreves tried to come in again as before, but Oracandus was ready. As the sword came at him, Kreves' wrist was grabbed, his arm yanked until he cried out. The sword fell on the ground.

Brandin rushed in and plowed into Oracandus again. They rolled around and nearly started another tumble down the hillside. Oracandus was raving and cursing. "Break your bones, crush your skull, eat your sweet flesh like all the others."

Oracandus twisted his head around so quickly that he was sinking his teeth into Brandin's arm before he could wrench loose. The pain was terrible. "Agh!" Grabbing a handful of the creature's matted hair he pulled back hard so that Oracandus had to let go. Blood poured from the bite marks. Brandin balled up his fist and struck his jaw. Then they tangled up again and rolled up next to a fallen tree. The two exchanged blow after blow. Oracandus continued ranting even when to do such cost him needed air. He was straining to keep moving after several minutes. Brandin struck him again. The blow sent Oracandus crashing into the tree, splintering the rotted wood around him. The smaller tree next to them cracked from the force.

Brandin, needing to catch his breath, pushed away and clambered up the hill to where his spear had fallen. Retrieving the God's Finger, he went to Kreves who was resting against a boulder. His face and hair were wet and he clutched his right arm.

"Are you okay?"

Kreves smiled. "Wrenched the arm from the socket. Got it back in, but I won't be swinging a sword anytime soon."

Brandin looked back down the slope. He could hear Oracandus thrashing around and attempting to get loose. Then he took a better look at the bite on his left shoulder. His coat was black with blood. It throbbed and burned but he was still able to handle the spear.

"Stay here," Brandin said.

Brandin didn't hear what Kreves said. He was already jogging down the hill. As he neared him, Oracandus burst out and locked eyes with him. "I'll speak a curse in the name of your father when I dine on your flesh, Stormbringer!"

Oracandus came at him like a frenzied bull.

Brandin leveled the spear and charged. The gap between them flashed away to nothing. As he struck, he was screaming just as loudly as Oracandus. The spear sliced through flesh, muscle, and bone until it protruded from the creature's back. In the same moment, Brandin cried out from the long gashes on his sides caused by Oracandus' claws. More unbelievable was the fact that he was still standing. The spear's head had missed the vital organs. Copious amounts of dark blood flowed out from the wound. Brandin struck Oracandus with his elbow and dragged the spear back out and shoved back with his foot.

He fell backward, the spear slipping out of his blood-wet hands. Oracandus was wailing again. The sound swelled up and seemed to be coming from every direction at once. His blood loss was taking its toll, but Brandin hoped that Oracandus' wound would fall him first. Rather than waiting around to find out, he scrubbed the blood from his fingers with dried leaves and moss. He snatched up the spear and did the same. Then Oracandus charged him again, his breathing ragged, his eyes engorged in his head, blood covering his chest.

The seconds passed slowly, Brandin was aware of every movement as he lifted the spear, noting Oracandus' approach, setting himself into a stance to hurl the weapon. He gritted his teeth and then the moment came. He pulled his arm back and flung the silver spear so that it seemed like a bolt of lightning. The crash of thunder happened when the force of the spear's impact flung Oracandus up against one of the larger rocks. The rock, thick limestone, was split from

142

top to bottom. The creature draped limply on the haft. Not moving. Not breathing. Blood oozed from the many wounds.

Oracandus was dead.

14

Bitter Victory

Brandin dabbed the sap from an herb growing along the stream on the bite and scratch marks. He'd spent some time cleaning them out in the water and hoped the bite would not fester. He glanced up at Oracandus's body, which was still pinned to the stone. Kreves was staring at it, muttering under his breath. He cradled his injured arm in a makeshift sling. Brandin resumed his treatment. It had been Kreves who pointed out the herb and its medicinal properties. He was also chewing on some sort of leave or a piece of tree bark that dampened pain.

The forest was so quiet now. The intensity of their battle gave way to deep weariness. Finishing with his work, Brandin stood up and climbed the hill to stand beside Kreves.

Kreves shook his head. "It's over. Ravenhold is no longer threatened. Natya is safe. Gods, Stormborn, you impaled him and embedded the spear into solid stone."

Brandin stretched his arm. A rivulet of blood made it through the layer of sap but there was little else. He glanced up into the boughs, trying to discern the level of the sun. It was certainly lower in the western sky. Then he looked at the corpse.

"He knew the gods had him marked for death, Kreves. And I was the one who executed their will. Me." He groaned. "Damn the gods. They got their way despite my resistance. That vile angeli is probably laughing his head off."

"Can the will of the gods truly be thwarted?"

Brandin looked at his friend now then shrugged. "I don't know anymore. Perhaps, my father will give me some answers."

Kreves popped another leaf into his mouth. "Do you think Valdan will tell you?"

Brandin scrubbed his hands across his face. "I hope so, Kreves. I hope so." His eyes found Oracandus again. "Do you want to make our way back to the others and the horses? Or make a camp and rest?"

"We might make it back to them before dark. I'll take my chances. I'm damned sure ready for that drink though."

Brandin smirked, though it slipped to a frown when his friend turned to collect his sword and other belongings. "Yeah. I'll buy the first round."

Oracandus smelled terrible and was getting worse in death. Brandin walked up to the body of the creature, and grabbed the spear by the haft and pulled it free from the stone and straight back through the body, which slid to the ground. He knelt and cleaned the tip the best he could. There was no damage at all that he could see. He looked again, taking more time to scan the shiny metal. The edge was perfect.

"What magic did this," he muttered.

"It's a god-crafted blade, Stormborn."

Brandin spun around, his spear held ready to let fly. He came face to face with a young woman, barely out of girlhood. She had blond hair combed back and tied with ribbons. She was dressed in a silken gown of pure white. The woman smiled. The same gods-cursed smile.

"You, but, you...," his words trailed off. His pent up anger was displaced by confusion. "Do you wear another form, angeli? Who is this poor girl?"

The woman smiled, broader now and her eyes twinkled with her mirth. "Dear, Brandin, this is my true form--or at least a mortal approximation. I've no need to hide behind other eyes now. I've finished my task. And so have you."

Anger was kindled. "Yes, I murdered Oracandus because the gods were too weak to act on their own."

The angeli stepped closer, her nose wrinkling at the corpse of the creature. She skirted wide of it and turned her too green eyes on Brandin. "Don't be a fool. There is always more going on than mortals can understand."

Brandin couldn't take his eyes off the angeli for a moment but then sought out Kreves. The man staring right at them, but it was as though he had been frozen in place.

"What did you do to him?"

The angeli waved away the question. "He is quite well. I only did that so we could speak freely. Mortals are not supposed to see me in most cases. When we are finished, he will move and not remember a thing."

"How comforting," muttered Brandin.

"Yes well, I just wanted to congratulate you on this *necessary duty*, Stormborn." Her face wrinkled in mock-seriousness. The gods are appeased, Oracandus, pathetic thing he was, can no longer make things difficult for Lord Dungray and his precious daughter. You are going to be a hero to the people once the myth-tellers get started and you will shine with the proper glory befitting one of the Stars. You even get something of a family reunion. It's a splendid turn of events, don't you think?"

Brandin didn't trust himself to answer. He stared at her, just a slip of a girl to his eyes, and he had trouble conjuring the will to strangle her. He had wanted to strike the messenger so much but now there was nothing but resentment towards his father's kind.

"Would that I could have an audience with the council of the gods in their abode," Brandin said. "I would give them the thanks they deserve for the gifts they have bestowed." His voice was thick with sarcasm. The angeli noticed certainly, but pretended he was serious.

"Oh, yes, indeed." Her unflappable smile deepened. "Yes, if only you had that chance." She laughed. "But that is not to be, Stormborn." She lowered her head but looked up at him. "At least not this time," she added with a certain teasing twist of her voice.

Brandin didn't bother asking what she meant. He'd had his fill of her and mischievous ways. "Go away, angeli. I have news to deliver. After that, I do not know what I shall do."

The angeli clutched her arms behind her back and smile again. The dimples in her cheeks were deep. She would have been fetching if Brandin didn't know what she was. "Oh, you will, though. Perhaps, it will come to you, Stormborn. Farewell for now."

One moment, the angeli was standing there radiating light, the next she had vanished. The glow departed and Kreves was moving again.

"So, are you ready," he asked

Brandin looked at Oracandus. "I am going to bury him."

Kreves stared at the corpse. "I'll help you."

"Thank you, Kreves."

The spot in front of the stone was slightly lower than the surrounding ground. Brandin looked up at the split stone still covered with Oracandus' blood.

"We'll cover him in a tomb of stones."

While Kreves curled the body up on its side, Brandin hefted a few fair-sized stones and set them up in a ring around it. Then he climbed rocks behind and heaved on the stones until they came loose. The stone weight a tremendous amount but Brandin was able to maneuver it enough to set it on top of Oracandus like the cap on a sarcophagus. When they were finished, both men stood in front of the tomb.

"I couldn't leave the body to the elements and the beasts," said Brandin.

"I don't completely understand the reasons, but I respect your choice. Let's be gone from this cursed place."

They made their way back down the stream, keeping the retreating light to their back. The darker it grew, the slower their progress. After perhaps two hours of steady hiking, Brandin realized he couldn't see much further than a hundred paces forward.

"We need to stop, Kreves. I prefer to not twist my ankle on these rocks or get a bath in the stream."

Kreves sipped from his canteen. "You'll get no argument from me. Let's make a fire before it's too dark."

They had a dinner of their rations around a roaring fire that chased away the autumn chill in the winds that whistled through the deep forest. Brandin's sleep was fitful. There were strange dreams in which the angeli smiled at him but her teeth were all bloody and jagged like she was devouring him, and Oracandus appeared to him in the form of an ordinary man dressed in a white cloak.

The next morning, he and Kreves set out as soon as there was enough light to negotiate the trail safely. Not long into the day, they came to the sheltering stones. The coals were still smoldering beneath a thin layer of dirt.

"Looks like Barring the others went back to the horses."

"Let's keep moving," said Brandin.

A few hours later, they came to the place where they had left the horses. Brandin caught the smell of cook fires. A few steps up the hill, a soldier stepped out of hiding.

"Captain Kreves, sir. Glad you are back." He glanced at Brandin. "Has the monster been killed?"

Kreves sighed. "Yes, we were successful. Where is Commander Barring?"

"He's eating breakfast, sir."

"Good. Take us up. I want to get the horses ready to ride out as soon as he is ready."

"Yes, Captain." The soldier saluted and went about his business.

Brandin continued up into the camp, walking a few steps behind Kreves. They were reunited with the remains of the party. Seven soldiers had lost their lives hunting Oracandus. The camp was set inside a clump of trees. Commander Barring was being aided to stand when they stepped inside the sheltering ring of sycamores. A tripod was dangling over the fire with a small cauldron boiling on it. The smells pouring from it were heavenly and made Brandin's mouth water.

He exchanged a look with Kreves that ended in a smirk.

He wiped the expression away when he saluted to Barring. "Glad you made it back here, Commander."

Barring saluted. "Seems you and Brandin Stormborn were able to end the threat with only minor injuries."

"Yes. I may not swing a sword for a while, but I'm still breathing."

Barring looked at Brandin. "We are grateful for your service, Master Stormborn. I lost men to the beast before and I am sad that more good soldiers had to die to bring Oracandus down."

"I did what needed to be done, Commander Barring. Now Ravenhold is secure. I would like to be out of the forest as soon as possible so we can share the news with Lord Dungray."

"Yes. Would you like to have breakfast first?"

"Indeed, we would, Commander," said Kreves.

15

A Grateful Lord

When they rode out of the darkness of the forest and into the full light of the sun and open country, Brandin sighed his relief. The remains of the party rode out into broader grasslands and pastures broken by only small clumps of trees and soon returned to the road. To the east, Ravenhold's towers were in sight. Brandin wondered if they had repaired the western gate into the city.

"Might be better to just take the long way around again. No telling how much progress they've made clearing the debris on this side." Kreves rode beside him and seemed to read his mind.

Brandin smiled. "I suppose it's fine. I'd rather avoid those tangles. I sort of like being out and away from all of the trees. The open country suits me better. The open sea," Brandin stopped and looked wistfully towards the distant coast. "The sea, best of all. I'm ready to sail away from Belandria. Maybe I'll return home for a spell."

"It is finished, isn't it? I can say that I rode with Brandin Stormborn and defeated a foul beast with him."

Brandin's grin turned sour. "Stories for the songsmiths to write poetic verses about, you mean."

Kreves shrugged. "Who knows? Maybe once we return, Lord Dungray will have a feast and the songsmith will be there too."

His friend was buoyant and acted like a boy surviving his first battle. Branding patted the stallion's neck absently and mused long on the angeli's cryptic words, now returned to his mind in the quietness of reflection. They retraced the same route back around the city on the south side and made decent time. Kreves kept them at a steady, albeit slower pace, to accommodate Commander Barring's injuries. The sense of dire urgency was absent. Everyone was anxious to return home and rest. Though men were killed, every soldier would grieve in his own way.

Brandin glanced back at Commander Barring. The man was pale and withdrawn. His injuries were worse than anyone's, his losses the worse. Six men had been killed by Oracandus during an ambush. Kreves, despite his experience as a soldier and leader of men, seemed blind to the costs. He only saw the glory they would garner. More reasons to hate the pull he had over the man.

It's all your fault, Brandin bloody Stormborn!

He was too weary to hold onto bitterness. One of the first things he would do when they returned to Ravenhold was sleep on a proper bed again. The drink with Kreves would have to wait. There would be time later and he was likely right about Dungray holding some feast in his honor. Word would spread even more widely than it already had about him being there. Legends would grow from the dirty truth.

Around midday, Brandin and the others were on one of the trade roads, trotting behind a caravan of merchant wagons, loaded with all manner of merchandise destined for the city markets. The party kept to itself, though they were hardly nondescript in the silver armor with the Dungray crest visible in the sun. Some of the merchant guards traded quips with the soldiers and someone mentioned his name in passing. That set off a flurry of questions and pointing fingers. A murmur cascaded from one end of the caravan to the other.

Everyone was talking about him and their quest in the forest.

"Just like that. Seems I can't escape the glory the gods want for those they claim as their own." Brandin frowned. "Damn the gods," he muttered, more out of habit than with any heat in it.

Kreves did nothing to put the murmurs to rest. He was smiling about it all. "You need to cheer up. We're alive, Stormborn. We could have ended up in Oracandus' belly, by the gods. You've got to admit that at least. No matter what part the gods played in this, you did what needed to be done to protect Natya and Ravenhold too. You did well."

Brandin wanted to grumble and argue but nodded instead. There was nothing good to be gained for dwelling on the results. For another hour or so, the party rode along with the caravan but as the walls of the city grew closer, Kreves signaled for them to ride fast. Soon, Brandin and the others were galloping hard for the final miles. The gates were already opening to receive them. As they passed through, the ring of their hooves on the cobblestone streets echoed everywhere. Then all was swallowed up by the noise of the people going about their business in the crowded streets. The thoroughfares were so clogged that they had to shout their way through and let the horse push when necessary. The people parted slowly, most hurrying when they realized who was coming.

"Make way," Kreves shouted. He stood up in the stirrups and pitched his voice louder. "Make way, I say!"

The crowded pushed and shoved each other to clear a path for the soldiers. No one noticed him. Perhaps the same people who had tossed rotten fruit at him two days ago, no just glanced at him in passing before moving about their business.

"Quite a different entrance, isn't it?"

When the merchants arrived further back, word spread like a wildfire up through the masses so that he was again hearing his name on the tongues of many by the time they were crossing the threshold of the citadel. Brandin felt the iron-studded gates slam home behind him and had a strange sense of foreboding come over him. He was reminded of the moments just before a charge on the battlefield was called.

They rode into the courtyards and went directly to the stables. Grooms were waiting to take their horses away. Brandin climbed down from the stallion, his behind sore from the riding, the rest of his body like one giant bruise.

Maybe a hot bath and some sleep in a comfy bed. Then drinks with Kreves.

He stretched his back and shoulder, trying to loosen the taut muscles. Brandin then noticed the grooms were bowing. He turned and saw that Lord Dungray had arrived. Kreves and the other soldiers were down on one knee and Brandin bowed his head but otherwise remained standing where he was. Dungray's face was sweaty, his skin ashen.

Something's wrong, Brandin realized.

Dungray approached, his personal guards were arrayed around him but he waved them back. "No, I will not hide like a child behind her mother's skirts."

"My lord, what is it," asked Brandin. From the corner of his eye, he saw Kreves stand.

"I'm so sorry, Stormborn. I...I sent a bird to Highcastle. I wanted the king to know who you were and explain what you were doing for Ravenhold." Dungray wiped the sweat away. "Did you succeed," he asked imploringly.

"Yes. Oracandus is gone now. Natya is free. Ravenhold is safe."

Dungray nodded, slowly, thoughtfully. "Thank you, Stormborn. Thank you so much. Gods, this is too much to bear."

"What, my lord? What is wrong? What news from Highcastle?" Kreves' eyes were locked on Dungray.

Dungray smiled, a weak, trembling twitch of the mouth. "The king has ordered me to detain you in Ravenhold so you might stand trial for your crimes as Brandell Shay. While he appreciates Brandin's efforts to make reparations, the crimes cannot be so easily forgiven."

"But, my lord Dungray, you cannot do this. This is Brandin Stormborn, son of Valdan the Stormbringer. He's... he's...," Kreves trailed off.

"Just a man, Kreves."

"No. You're more than a man."

Dungray looked around at the servants gathered about them. "And I am a Belandrian noble and one who is loyal to his king. I am sorry but I must obey."

Brandin guessed something. "You did not tell the king about Natya's part in this, did you?"

Dungray tried to compose himself. His voice was stiff. "No. No, I didn't."

Brandin nodded. "Better for you to keep that out of it." He rolled his head to ease the pain in his neck. "What now?"

Lord Dungray thought for a moment. "I will not post guards on you. You are free to move about the citadel but not leave. I am having a feast no matter what comes. You deserve that much, Stormborn. Please take time to rest. I will have servants at your call."

"Thank you, my Lord. You are honorable at heart."

The noble had no response but started to leave. At that point, Natya came out into the yard. She found Brandin and gasped. Her eyes flooded with tears. "You are safe," she managed through sobbing, though she also smiled.

Brandin felt his face flush. Everyone was looking from him to Natya. Almost everyone, that is. Kreves was already turning away and walking off, his face pointed towards the ground.

"Yes. Back in one piece. There is no more need to worry about Oracandus."

Natya's smile faltered. "Then you will go now."

Brandin winced. "Not exactly. Seems I must bow to the king's justice."

"What," asked Natya. "Father, what is he talking about? You were going to let him go on his way, all of his transgressions forgiven."

"I was, my dear. Truly I was. But the king bids me to keep him at Ravenhold until arrives. Two days more and the royal entourage will be in the city."

"No. Brandin should be rewarded not punished. He's done so much to make amends. Father, please don't."

Lord Dungray's face trembled. A war raged inside the man. Brandin knew it. He felt the pain of choice just as surely.

"I must obey the king, Natalya."

Natya was weeping now and fled the courtyard. Brandin ached inside and wanted to follow after her, but kept his feet planted there on the ground. His own emotions were twisted by the sight of the girl. He cared about Natya.

The awkward lull caused by the outburst became too much. Lord Dungray stalked off with his guards leaving Brandin with the soldiers who were deeply confused by what happened. Commander Barring was helped off his horse and taken away to Dungray's healers. The grooms took the horses. The soldiers dispersed so that only Kreves and he remained.

"Kreves, what is it?"

His friend stood several paces away, cradling his injured arm. "Don't worry about it. I'm sure you want a bath and maybe I can get one of the servants to bring up some ointments for your injuries. The herbs have dealt with the worst of it."

Brandin looked hard at Kreves. He expected him to put up more of a fight and protest Dungray's decision with more vigor. The man looked resigned. Brandin followed after him. He felt a strange disquiet, a sense that something was about to happen. Something possibly dangerous.

A cold gust of wind blew through the courtyard. Brandin shivered and clutched at the ragged sleeve of his ruined coat. *I'll have to see about some new clothes. If I am going to die, I'd rather not be wearing rags.*

Brandin was taken straight to the room he had in Dungray's family apartments. Isla was waiting. She gave a deep curtsy and smiled. "Ready to serve you, Master Stormborn."

Kreves dismissed her. "Just have the others prepare a hot bath. Bring us wine in the meantime."

"Yes, Captain Kreves," said Isla.

In a short time, Brandin was sitting at the couch, boots and stockings discarded, coat tossed into the far corner of the room. His shirt was ripped and bloodstained. His eyes were closed and a slight smiled cropped up. "This feels just wonderful. I'd had enough of the hard ground."

Kreves was sitting in a high-backed chair, his fingers busily tapping the table next to it. He had a look of intense concentration on his face. His friend looked worn out and in need of a good shave and bathe himself. The man was also annoying him at the moment.

"What is it, damn you?"

Kreves pounded the table. "So you're just going to accept your fate? Let the king decide whether you live or die?"

"What should I do? I don't have that many options. I can't just open the citadel gates and walk out of Ravenhold."

Kreves stood up, wincing when he wrenched his right arm. "I don't know. This just doesn't seem right."

"Right or wrong, I have to face the king's judgment," said Brandin.

"But, is that the will of the gods?"

"Will of the gods, Kreves? The bloody will of the gods. What of their will? Thinking there is any <i>one will among them is madness. Damn them all. I may have the chance to speak with my father again, but I won't let that change my opinion so easily."

Damn you too, angeli!

"Then what's the point to anything? Is there no place for faith, then? You've already heard me say that I have faith in you, Brandin. I want to believe that you live for a purpose and that what you do inspires others. Mankind is better when the Stars shine and light the way."

Brandin looked at his friend. He believed so strongly, with all of his heart. "Kreves, I...." A knock at the door interrupted him.

"Come in," said Kreves.

Isla entered the room with a platter laden with food and drink. As she sat it down, Kreves grabbed a cup and poured the wine. He stood up and carried the cup to Brandin. He handed it to him and looked at him with such a pained expression that Brandin could do little more than say thanks in a weak voice. When his wine was poured, Kreves returned to his seat.

Isla prepared the lunch for them and left not long afterward. The two of them ate in silence for a time. The food was welcome enough that they put aside their quarrel. They feasted on pickled eggs, fried bread topped with jelly and apple butter, sliced ham covered with glazed brown sugar.

Another servant arrived to say that the bathwater was ready. Brandin and Kreves left the room and went to the expansive bath chambers with its four enormous copper tubs heated by stoves. One wall was lined with mirrors and built-in washbasins made of polished stone. The steam from the hot water made the air hazy but immediately made Brandin feel slightly better. He went about removing his clothes and sank slowly into the tub.

Kreves stood there for a moment just inside the doorway. "I'll be back later, Stormborn."

Brandin nodded and watched his friend leave. Then he

closed his eyes and submerged his head in the soothing waters to saturate his dirty hair. The aches and pains faded in the time he sat in the heat and steam. Once his skin was completely wrinkled he stepped out, toweled off, and went to the mirrors. A razor and cup filled with frothy cream were there. Wiping the moisture off the mirror he set about shaving the beard that was growing in. Afterward, he dressed and looked around for his boots. He remembered he'd left them in his rooms. He looked down at the soiled clothes and scrunched up his nose.

"I don't want to put those back on," he said aloud.

Only then did he see the robe sitting on a chair. He looked around and decided to put it on. He went to the bath chamber door and cracked it open. No one was standing guard outside. Dungray had kept his word. Hitching the robe about his waist tighter, Brandin entered the hall and walked the short distance back to his room.

Inside, he found a new set of clothes spread out over his bed. New boots and stockings were set over near the couch. Brandin opened his mouth but there was no one to thank. Ilsa had been in to collect the dirty dishes and must have disposed of the boots as well. He smiled and set about dressing. He stopped short of pulling on his boots or putting on his coat. Brandin dropped onto the bed. The softness of the pillows and mattress took him in a matter of moments. He was snoring loudly and deeply asleep. Thus, he did not notice the pale-haired girl garbed in a white silken gown lounging in the chair a mischievous grin twisting her lips.

16

Where Loyalties Lie

S tormborn, wake up."

Brandin stretched out on the soft bed then opened his eyes very slowly. The room was lit by lamplight. Kreves was standing over him, looking clean and refreshed. He wore a gray dress jacket with silver thread woven into the arms and along the bottom. His right arm was in a fresh sling tied around his neck.

"What is it," Brandin asked groggily.

"It's time for the feast. Lord Dungray sent me up to collect you. Let's go." Kreves was brusque and had a sour look on his face. "Last bloody meal you'll have as a free man, I'll wager."

Brandin ignored his jab and rolled off the bed and went to the couch. He dragged on his new stocking and the fine leather boots. Once he'd checked his hair in the mirror to make sure it wasn't a big tangle after his nap, he put on the new woolen coat, which was died red and covered with embroidered scrollwork along the sleeves. Again he admired himself in the mirror. They were the finest clothing he had ever worn.

"Alright. You look lovely, not a hair out of place. Let's go, Stormborn."

Brandin snorted. "Lead on. Just stop being an ass."

Kreves stiffed at the remark, his shoulders hunching up. He stopped. "Me being an ass? What about you?" He came up to him, within a pace and looked at him. He had slight wrinkles at the corners of his eyes. "Brandin. Let's leave now. I can find a way to get you out of the citadel."

Brandin considered his friend. "Kreves, we wouldn't get past the guards no matter what you said or did. The only thing that would do was get you clapped in chains for helping me escape. No. We have to see this through."

Kreves pounded the doorframe with his left fist. He gritted his teeth but reined in his words. "Fine. We will do it your way. Maybe you won't but I'll be praying to Valdan from this point forward."

Brandin felt his stomach lurch but kept his face smooth. "If that makes you feel better."

They left the room and headed out away from the Dungray apartments down through the corridors guarded at all times by the elite soldiers. After several turnings, Brandin heard the faint sounds of music. Kreves took him in a new direction into another part of the citadel and the songs and merriment became more pronounced so that he could make out the words of the songs being sung. They came to a broad corridor. The floor was patterned in colored tiles and the columns were richly engraved with images of the gods and other creatures of legend and lore.

Brandin walked beside Kreves now. The soldiers lining the entrance hall saluted both of them as they neared the doors to the dining hall. Those doors, made of some dark metal, were open wide to receive them. He could see circles of dancers moving within, servants burdened with platters of food and wine. The music from flutes, mandolins, and drums flowed and echoed back from the tall ceiling.

There were other guests inside as well. Dungray had invited certain members of Ravenhold's wealthy and influential citizens to the feast, no doubt. Brandin entered the hall and saw that a series of tables had been set up to accommodate everyone. Fires burned in both hearths, one on each end of the long, narrow room. Near one of the fireplaces, sat Dungray and Natya as well as Commander Barring. There were two empty chairs at the main table. Kreves was headed directly over there. The music was swelled louder, with a pair of maidens singing in bright and clear voices. Brandin looked around at the guests, dressed in all of their finery, and wondered how many knew what lay in store for him or what he had done to merit a feast.

A servant passed him carrying a platter steaming with hot mutton and new potatoes. His mouth watered. He hadn't eaten for some time and decided he would enjoy himself for the time being. He would not dwell on the decision of the king before it was made, tempting though it was. He smiled at the man, dressed in the Dungray livery, and walked the final paces to the table. He eyed Natya, who sat composed and wearing a beautiful blue gown. Her raven black hair was bejeweled with pearls and amethyst, linked by thin chains. She looked at him, tried to smile but ended up frowning. Next to her, Lord Dungray nodded. The noble wore a black velvet tunic with embroidered stags encircling the ends of the sleeves.

"Welcome, Stormborn," said Dungray. "I hope you like

the feast I've prepared."

Brandin bowed in respect. "Thank you, my lord. It all looks, sounds, and smells so wonderful."

"This is the least I could do considered all that I owe you." Dungray met his gaze steadily. "The least. I hope I might be able to do more. Please sit down. Captain, you may sit next to Stormborn. You are being honored here tonight as well for your part. The same for Commander Barring." Dungray gestured to the man sitting to the right of Natya.

"Thank you, Lord Dungray," said Barring. He nodded his head in lieu of bowing.

Kreves, still standing, bowed. "Thank you, my lord."

Once they were both in chairs, wine was brought to them immediately. Before Brandin could take a sip, Lord Dungray stood up. As though waiting for the motion, musicians were quieted and the guests stopped their murmuring.

"May I have your attention, friends. We're gathering here today to honor brave men who faced a demonic threat not far beyond the walls of this city. Only a few of you knew about the creature Oracandus and his attacks on our people. He was a threat to all of us." He turned to Brandin before continuing. "By luck or providence, an answer was delivered to us in the form of this man: Brandin Stormborn."

The guests gawked and gaped, and a buzz of whispers filled the hall.

"Yes," Dungray continued. "One of the Stars has fallen in our midst, dear friends. A strange turn of events considering that he played such a fateful and terrible part in our history. Some of you know that he first came to us as Brandell Shay, a notorious criminal according to many." He looked down at his wine glass. "And to me. He came here willingly when he could have easily freed himself. He showed himself to be not the debased monster that many of us thought he was but rather a man of honor. He put himself in harm's way to save my life when we faced zeranths on the grasslands. Then he when heard of our plight concerning Oracandus he chose to save us. For that and more I have forgiven him for the past losses. Let us make a toast to Brandin Stormborn."

All across the hall, the guests took up glasses of wine. Beside Brandin, Kreves held aloft his glass.

"To Brandin Stormborn, we the citizens of Ravenhold are indebted and grateful for your timely intervention." Dungray took the first drink and the others followed. Then the noble sat down and the music resumed and the servants continued plying the guests with more food and drink.

Leaning closer to Dungray, Brandin spoke softly. "Thank you. I do not deserve your forgiveness but I accept it. I only hope the king shows similar mercy."

Dungray took another drink of wine, gulping it down quickly. He looked over at Brandin. "Yes, if it comes to that I hope so too."

"What do you mean, my lord?"

Dungray smiled. "Never mind that now. Please eat, drink, and enjoy yourself."

Brandin didn't press him further but sat back and drank more wine. A platter of mutton and potatoes was set down before him. He licked his lips and let questions go to enjoy the succulent repast. The feast continued into the night, with several courses of dinner coming from the kitchens in succession. Brandin ate roasted quail, beef stew heaped with potatoes, carrots and onions, and a variety of sticky pastries topped with gooseberry sauce.

Although he tried to speak with Natya, she remained aloof most of the time. Dungray noticed but said very little about it. Instead occupied Brandin with stories of his military campaigns, his time at the great university in Highcastle, and with the exploits of his deceased brother. The latter, Brandin was sure, was intended to show him that he was truly ready to move past his involvement in Lord Wilsley's demise. Dungray's cheeks and nose were rosy with too much wine. He spoke in long, meandering rambles. Brandin didn't mind. He was feeling rather warm with drink himself.

At one point, Dungray leaned in, clapping him on the back. "You know, Stormborn, I was going to mention this afterward, but decided to say it now." He smiled. "I think I will let you leave Ravenhold."

Brandin blinked, trying to think through the haze of liquor. "What of the king? Won't you be punished for letting me go?"

Dungray swallowed more wine, tapping his tongue several times afterward. He looked ready to fall over right there. He smiled again. "Maybe. But I don't care, Stormborn. You saved us. You saved my little girl." His eyes sparkled with tears and his mouth puckered. "I owe you that. Think on what I've said."

With that, Dungray turned away and spoke to Natya quietly so he could not hear over the flutes and drums. It was as though Brandin had imagined the exchange. On his other side, Kreves was sitting his wine. He no longer looked angry. A jaw-cracking yawn escaped him just then.

"Tired?"

Kreves snorted. "I didn't take a long nap like you did this afternoon. I had duties to perform all over the citadel. There

168

were reports to be filed and I had to listen to the city watch leaders complain about the state of the clean up from the riots and the fires. So yes, I'm bloody tired." He arched his eyebrow. "But this is damned good wine and I'm going to savor it."

Brandin agreed. He took up a glass. It blurred in front of his eyes so he saw three glasses instead of one. Kreves did the same. "Cheers." As they sipped their wine, Brandin nearly mentioned Dungray's comment but decided against it. *Let the morning and a sober mind tell me the truth of things.*

The feasting and drinking finally ended and the last thing Brandin remembered was Kreves dragging him along the corridor to his room. When he awoke the next morning, his head was clouded and pounding. Wincing with the pain, Brandin stayed abed for some time. His eyes were burning and the urge to sick up was strong. For a wonder, no one bothered him. Sometime around midday, he slid out of the bed and sat on the couch. He had slept in his clothes so they were rather wrinkled. Not long after, a small rap at the door brought him up.

"Come in," he said.

Lord Dungray walked in. He was drinking some odd-smelling drink from a cup. The steam wafted through the cool air. "Hello, Stormborn."

Brandin was on his feet. He blinked several times. "Lord Dungray. I wasn't expecting to see you."

"I wasn't expecting to be here either. Drank too damned much wine last night. If my Lidia were alive she would have stopped me long before I made a fool out of myself."

"You weren't the only fool last night, my lord," said Brandin.

Dungray nodded. "Yes, well, be that as it may, I am here drinking this foul concoction. Nasty but effective at dealing with the effects of too much drink."

"Why are you here?"

Dungray walked in and sat down on the chair. "What I am about to say did not happen. Do you understand?"

Brandin rubbed his eyes. "Maybe."

"Stormborn, I remember what I said to you last night. Do you?"

Brandin frowned. Then it came back to him. "You said you wanted to let me leave Ravenhold. I am surprised that you remembered though. You were several drinks ahead of me."

"Yes, well, I remember and I haven't changed my mind about it. I am letting you go. I've had both my daughter and Captain Kreves talking with me and pleading. Never mind my own guilt and misgivings. The heart of the matter is that I do not have malice towards you any longer. I had my own ideas about the sort of man you were when all I could see was Brandell Shay. I cannot let you pay for crimes that may have been justified."

Brandin started to argue. "Surely, you can't believe that. My lord, I--"

Dungray cut him off with a raised hand. "Let me finish. There are problems with how we nobles have managed the affairs of the kingdom and its people, down to the lowest born. Maybe my brother was part of the problem or just unlucky. I believe now that you were acting with the same honorable intentions you've displayed since I met you. That counts for a great deal in my estimation. The king does not know you. His only concerns will be pursuing the letter of law to appease factions that harbor animosity over the effects of the Casteny Revolt."

"But, I did break the law, didn't I?"

Brandin waited for Dungray to drink from the steaming cup.

"Technically, yes. But I believe you upheld a far higher law, and for that, I am letting you go. However, there is a small problem. If I do, I may likely be punished in no small way. I doubt even the influence of a House as old and as well connected as mine could spare me that much."

Brandin was confused. "You could be sentenced to death."

Dungray waved that away. "No, not that severe. And not if you let me explain the plan."

"The plan," said Brandin. "What plan?"

"Captain Kreves has decided to leave my service and will be secreting you out of the city under cover of night. I will wholly unaware and will take measures to see that you are pursued as escaped criminals."

"He what?" Brandin's head was spinning. "You can't be serious. Why would he do it?"

Dungray smiled. "He is a loyal man. Was always one of my best soldiers. Meeting you changed him. His devotion to you was beyond question when we spoke. He means to spirit you away. I've directed him to the docks in the port of Gelestad. You can book passage on one of the ships owned by my family. Kreves will have documents to get you aboard. They are *forged* papers."

"I don't know what to say."

"There is no need," said Dungray. "I only ask that you accept this offer." He got up and headed to the door, pausing just outside in the hall. "One more thing. My daughter is smitten with you, Stormborn. I do not blame her. I ask you to speak to her."

When Dungray was gone, Brandin sat on the couch, his mind reeling from the turning of his luck. He felt overcome by Kreves' sacrifice. He needed to speak with him. Then he thought of Natya.

"That will be the hardest part."

17

Return to the Sea

Brandin went in search of Natya, hoping he could speak with her before he talked to Kreves. There was much to say and likely not much time left. There were only a few hours until nightfall and he had no idea yet when he and Kreves would make their escape. The risks were low for the first part. No one would question Kreves if he were escorting him. The trouble would start when the king's forward guards became aware of his disappearance. They would likely have the whole night and part of the following day. Brandin mused on these things as he went first to Natya's room.

He waited while word was sent inside and only after he'd spent twenty minutes waiting did one of the maidservants tell him Natya wasn't there and that she had gone to one citadel's small garden. Not knowing the whole layout of the buildings, Brandin roved the corridors begging directions from the servants that he met along the way. Since there were four gardens spread across the grounds, they were only of limited help in his quest. Brandin passed guards too and he could tell that some were not as awed by him as those like Kreves. Some of the men were short with him and he could tell they were trying to rein in their feelings. They only saw Brandell Shay, a man responsible for many deaths. These men, perhaps from the same commoner families who lost sons, husbands, and fathers, were gruff and far less forgiving than Lord Dungray. Brandin could only mutter his thanks for their likely spurious directions and keep moving.

Where is she?

Just as he rounded another corner, he came to a passage that smelled of fresh air and flowers. He followed the aromas until he felt a slight breeze on his face. Brandin jogged down the hall, ignoring the stares of both servants and soldiers, and went through two sets of doors. Each was open to let in the cool, autumn air. He stepped through the last doors and into the open air. The rock paths at the bottom of the stairs spread out like the spokes of a wheel in five directions away from him. Trees, bushes, fruit bushes, and late-blooming flowers filled the garden so that the walls of the citadel were sometimes hidden from view.

Brandin took one of the paths at random and followed it for a few minutes. He came across smaller paths that led to rock gardens and stone benches etched with flower patterns and invocations to the gods. Even a statue appeared here and there to denote a shrine to one of the Ten Known Gods. He found himself thinking of his father, looking at the statues he passed a little more closely in case he happened upon a shrine to the Stormbringer. At another smaller intersection, he left one of the main spokes and followed the path as it wound through a tiny grove of apple trees flush with the red fruit. Brandin picked one from a low-hanging branch and saw the head of a statue up ahead.

He heard the voices before he saw to whom they belonged. Low, furtive prayers. Then he saw the lightning bolt in the statue's hand. Brandin's mouth twisted but he rounded a small hedge wall that encircled the statue to provide privacy for visitors to the shrine. A guard stood at the entrance. He looked at Brandin and glanced inside. Brandin looked and saw it was Natya. She was kneeling on a cushion, her long black hair loose and flowing down her back.

The guard cleared his throat. "My lady?"

Natya glanced back. Her eyes widened when she saw Brandin.

Brandin bowed his head. "May I speak to you?"

Natya nodded silently. He entered the small alcove before the shrine. The sound of birdsong and the breeze marked the only sounds for a time as they both stared up at the chiseled features of the god.

"What is it, Brandin?" Natya's voice was so soft. She was looking at him now. Her eyes were radiant with this beatific glow. She was so stunning. Brandin felt the urge to kiss her glistening lips.

Lowering his eyes to look at the stones, Brandin struggled a few moments to get the words out. In the end, he decided on simplicity though he was rather conflicted. He lowered his voice and bent closer so the guard would not hear so easily. "I am leaving, Natya. Kreves is getting me out of Ravenhold tonight. Your father is turning a blind eye so that we might have a chance."

"Did I get the chance to thank you for what you did? For saving me in that inn? For trying to help me get away even when you had no idea who I was or what was wrong?"

"Yes, my lady, you did. But you are more than welcome. I only did what I thought was right."

Natya put her hand on his. "And what if I said the same thing? What if I said that the right thing was for me to leave with you and Captain Kreves? What if I said that I couldn't bear to be apart from you, Brandin Stormborn?"

Brandin's stomach fluttered. "I would say that you must check your heart with your mind, my lady. For we barely know one another."

"Am I not desirable? Or am I not worthy of a starchild?"

Brandin smiled. "You are very beautiful. And you are more than worthy, Natya. But I cannot let you throw your life here in Belandria away. I cannot provide the safety and security that you deserve." He sighed. "I will not offend your honor or that of your father."

Natya nodded. Her lips pursed. "May I kiss you just this once? To say thanks, one more time, for what you have done for me and my city?"

Brandin hesitated but nodded. Natya tipped her head up and looked into his eyes. Slowly, Brandin leaned in and touched his lips to hers. The kiss was brief but left his skin tingling all over.

"Gods," he whispered. Natya tried to grab him but he gently moved her away. She looked at him with fresh tears glistening in her eyes. Brandin tried to speak but had to clear his throat. "Goodbye, Natya."

"Will you return to Belandria?"

"I don't know," said Brandin. "Natya, I am sorry that I cannot give you a better answer."

Natya nodded, wiping the moisture from her cheeks. "Be safe, Brandin. I will pray to the Stormbringer for you."

Brandin stood up, looked at the statue, and smirked. "Yes. Perhaps he will listen." Natya stood but remained where she was, hands clasped in front of her. Brandin touched her shoulder and moved out of the alcove.

He left the shrine behind and moved up the paths until he could see the open doors just beyond a row of hedges. His heart was thundering and his skin still tingled as he went back inside the citadel. Instead of searching for Kreves, Brandin returned to his room and stayed there to wait. He was sure the man would eventually come to him. Not long after he sat on the couch, Ilsa came in with a tray of wine.

"Would you like some refreshment, Master Stormborn?"

Brandin sat forward, elbows propped on his knees. "Thank you, Ilsa." He watched the servant set the tray on the table and turn to go. "Isla?"

"Yes."

"Can you send word to Captain Kreves that I am waiting in my room?"

"I will. Anything else?"

"No. That is all." Brandin smiled. "Thank you."

Ilsa left and Brandin went to the table and poured himself a cup of wine. His head was still fuzzy from the feast and his parting with Natya. He sipped with wine and resumed his place on the couch. The time went by and the sunlight faded. When full night had fallen Kreves knocked on the door then entered.

"Stormborn, are you ready?" Kreves paused on the threshold. "Are you in here still? I can't see a gods-cursed thing."

"I'm here, Kreves." He drained the last of the wine from his cup. The empty pitcher was on the floor.

Kreves found the lamp and lit it from the brazier in the

room's small fireplace. A soft golden glow filled the room slowly until Brandin could see the shapes of the bed, the table, the chair, and Kreves watching him with his arms crossed.

"I've made preparations. We have a small amount of supplies, at least enough to get us to Gelestad. I have the documents we need to book passage aboard one of the trade ships at anchor there."

"Kreves, are you sure you want to do this? You're leaving everything behind you. Your life of service to the Dungrays? Your status and rank?"

The lamplight was bright enough for him to see Kreves's face. Brandin recognized the stubborn set of his jaw. "I meant it when I said the words to Lord Dungray. I am sure. I'm a captain no more, Stormborn. I will do my best to get you back to the sea and well away from the hand of the king. Where we go from here, I do not know, but I want to be with you. I've made that decision, understanding the consequences."

Brandin felt light-headed from the wine. He wasn't going to argue with Kreves and felt a small relief that he would be traveling, at least for a time, with another person. "I believe you, my friend." He stood up. "Let's go then."

Leaving Ravenhold was a simple matter. Brandin let Kreves handle all of the talking as they passed through the various checkpoints of citadel security. With no official orders to restrain him, Brandin went from the stables on the same stallion while Kreves rode his favor mare. A third horse, packed with provisions for the journey to Gelestad, was pulled behind them. From the gates, they moved into the dark streets of the city proper where the flow of traffic had died down so that at certain points they were the only ones occupying the street. Kreves took an easterly route down the streets through various squares until they were waiting before the eastern gates themselves.

After Kreves show them who he was and showed him the papers supplied by Lord Dungray, they were riding through the tall doors and out into the open country. The skies were clear and filled with a rich tapestry of stars. The moon was a quarter full and lent its light to the world so they could move along slowly without fear of injuring the horses.

Brandin did not look back as the city disappeared over a bend in the country. Kreves was riding next to him, humming to himself. They lost themselves to the rhythm of the road, sticking to trade routes for the first leg of the journey and only leaving them when they were nearing the city of Sekland. Kreves angled off on one of the secondary roads and they were in the midst of farmland for a good twenty miles.

They were alone in the wide-open country until the land sloped downward and the road they were on merged again with a broader, better-maintained road. Occasionally, Brandin saw a lone seagull soaring on the current of the wind and he could again smell the familiar scent of the sea and it rejuvenated him as nothing had.

"We'll be in Gelestad by tomorrow morning if we ride till nightfall," said Kreves.

Brandin thought about his time in Belandria. He'd come to the kingdom with one set of expectations; one fate for himself in mind and now so much was different. He didn't know what to think. Perhaps, Valdan would provide the answers he sought. The thought led to a silent prayer, the first time he'd spoken to the god since he was a boy.

"Then we'll get to see where the wind blows us, Kreves.

It's sure to be an adventure. I hope you're ready."

"Of course I am. I'm sailing into the unknown with Brandin Stormborn by my side." Kreves smiled.

Brandin just laughed.

About the Author

SHAUN KILGORE is the author of various works of fantasy, science fiction, and a number of nonfiction works. His books appear in both print and ebook editions. He also has published numerous short stories and collections. Shaun lives in eastern Illinois. For more information, visit www.shaunkilgore.com.

Made in United States
North Haven, CT
28 November 2022

27459353R00114